Everybody
Lies

Table of Contents

For my Lowcountry family....

"Not all those who wander are lost."

J.R.R. Tolkien

Cindy
Barrineau
Curtis

---

1.   http://www.cindybcurtis.com

Chapter 1
Cue Up the Music

The lying begins. As the team manager, I scan my team's computer screens across the stark modern decor of our office space. So much effort is expended to look like the work assigned is not minimized under the social media posts, searches for Airbnb rentals, or how-to videos and reels. All of my team at Solid Solutions LLC navigates this balance with finesse and skill. I cue up Fleetwood Mac's "Little Lies" and hum it to myself as I try to focus on the job at hand.

Keyboards tap as strongly as a drum beat. I calm myself with the steady rhythm. The pings of alerts on cell phones and laptops add to the symphony. Inhale. Exhale. Another day begins in the office space that I supposedly manage.

The to-do list for today, written out before I left yesterday evening, waits for me to attack as soon as I sit down. I stand behind my designer chair and survey the room once again. Each carefully vetted employee moves ever so slightly from what they were doing to looking like they are truly working. I see this every day. Maybe if I worked standing, they would comply.

Clacinda breezes by my desk. Fresh outside air, mixed with coffee and creamer laced with local honey, follows her to her cubicle.

"Good morning, Ms.V! Just refilling my cup of Joe so I can work even harder for the good of us all!"

My parents named me Vinca. Yes, the flowers you plant every year that add a pop of color to your yard. Much easier to go by "V" instead of hearing all the flower innuendos. When I made manager of the team, "Ms. V" evolved in a weird sort of way.

"I hear ya!" I air high-five her coffee cup as she slips by me in her second-hand patterned skirt and office flats.

"So impressed that someone is working hard for the good of us all," I mumble, one of my secret stash of remarks to sustain me in times of high stress.

Our all-woman-run company consults with clients on ways to effectively solve problems in their businesses. Respect that, please. As the floor manager for ten of our employees, I wrangle, herd, group, encourage, and rage under my breath. I move people from point A to point finished on a continuum from one problem solved to another. We thrive on problems, which lends itself to a very unique work environment encased in and around little lies.

I have tried my best to calculate how many lies are told in the course of a day. Lies to each other, lies to our clients, lies to cover, and lies to expose, abound. They are so much a part of normal that no one even notices except me. I make a tally mark on my calendar notating lie one of this day. I get some kind of weird satisfaction from being right. I like to add them up at the end of the work week and see if we have made progress in any direction. I realize deciphering the lies is the biggest part of my job.

On a positive note, I worked smart to get my job! I impressed my interviewers by doing my research and asking the right questions. I let them know I am very competitive in a nurturing, tolerant way, and "she works well with others" was written on at least three of my report cards. I like to be responsible and to build a capable and confident team. My only problem is that everybody lies.

I people-watch as I work on my own tasks. Clacinda has returned to her desk after stopping to talk to each and every person on our team. From single moms to fresh-from-college grads with a degree in business to a retiree seeking a part-time job, my team is comprised of talented people. I notice the subtle shift from social media to work screen as smiles fade and brows furrow. By ten o'clock, the furrows deepen, and most of the team is honestly working. On a good day, we will buzz along until eleven thirty when the texts start circulating about where to eat, who has what to offer, and any office gossip that was not already delivered by Clacinda to us all.

My biggest client has let me know the fee for my services has been delivered to my account. That just makes me smile until I check the other messages and see the lies pop off the page. Yes, it has begun the payment process. No, it is not in my account. I tally this on another spreadsheet of lies from clients so as not to confuse my team tallies with my client tallies. Anger begins to travel from the pit of my stomach. The churning of my blood raises my pressure point. I begin to shallow breathe. The tallies of this week far exceed last week's. My cell phone alerts the boss ringtone.

"Vinca, here, how can I help you?"

"Hey, I need that report from last week ASAP. Did you not read your email?"

"No, I didn't." Better admit the hard truth than try to explain my tallies.

"I will get on that right away."

"You know, Vinca, I value you as team leader more than I can say; however, you have to follow protocol just like everyone else. 'Read your messages as soon as you arrive' sets the tone for the day. I expect better from you and that report by 2:00."

"Okay, on it, bye."

"What the heck?" I ask myself. She has no idea what I have been doing since I arrived or how I am managing my team! I open my messages and see her request, pull up the report that I thankfully finished before I left on Friday. I hit send, resisting the urge to bold the time in the subject box. I have got to get out of here and calm myself down, or I'm no good to anyone.

Our offices are on the second floor of a townhouse that is leased to small businesses. The lobby contains a comfortable waiting area where clients can check in for a person-to-person meeting. They buzz our central hub, and we take care of their needs. I pass through the open cheerful space after letting the team know I will lunch off campus and run errands. I need to be outside in the fresh air of autumn in the Lowcountry of South Carolina.

In our zone, we have a fall that teases and taunts before finally settling into itself. One day can be 60 degrees and the next 80. The leaves turn slowly, rather than one burst of color and done. The browns, rusts, and yellows slip in between the greens still lingering to make fall a mystery of sorts. Into this colorful landscape of pastel buildings against the indigo blue sky, I start walking around the town square to the sanctuary of the local green space park. My mind begins to ease. The steady rhythm of my feet on the pavement takes all the stress down a bit. I take a bite from my Honey Crisp apple, relishing the sweet tang and letting the calm begin to take effect.

The first bench I see is occupied by a young mom steadily typing into her cell phone as her sleeping baby sighs. "I wonder what lies she's telling?" crosses my mind as I walk on to the next free bench.

I ease back on the wooden bench slats and toss the core to the edge of the azalea bushes for the squirrels to enjoy. I begin to process my morning. I tilt my head against the bench back to better gaze into the deep blue, cloudless sky. I close my eyes for five minutes of peace. I hear a rustling of leaves first and then a soft squeal. My eyes open quickly and dart about. I see nothing and resume my eyes-closed-head-back-stance of peace. The squeal increases in volume and proximity to me. I recognize the distress call as that of a small feline. I jump up and follow the sound with no thought of what I will do when I locate the kitten. I don't even consider how my sassy cat, Georgie, would react to competition in the form of a feral kitten.

Right before I go off path, I glance at the young mother. She tightens a red belt around her middle. My mind is transformed back to ages ago.

"The shine on the vinyl was worn in some spots from the creasing of weight gained during another pregnancy and lost when the next baby arrived. The wide red belt worn over the more threadbare outfits added sass and style. The red, square buckle sat front and center when worn on the slender or not-so-slender woman/mom. A gold, slightly scarred prong fitted through the grommet to tighten or release the belt. The belt turned darker with more snap when it smacked my small legs."

I shake my head several times as if I can somehow erase the memory. A flash of orange tabby flits under a tree root. I follow, entranced between the memory and the reality of a distressed kitten.

"It's okay, little one. You can trust me," I softly speak as I stoop down to the edge of the tree's root where the tabby has hidden. I place my hand out, palm down, trying to coax the kitten out with my voice and calm presence.

My racing heart calms down in recovery. I put the red-belt-deep-dive where it belongs as the first item on my checklist of Everybody Lies."

Before the kitten gives me the time of day, an odor of soured playground hair, filled with sweat and weeks of unwashed oil, permeates the air. I resist the urge to hold my nose, will my heart to slow down, and turn my head to look over my right shoulder. The source of the odor stands in my circle. I can't tell the gender, but I can tell the last time this person bathed. A once tan trench coat covers every bit of the body from the shoulder to the mid calf. A pair of ratty tennis shoes peeks out from the edges of tattered jeans. Not the torn at exactly the right spot fashion jeans of today, but the torn edges from miles of walking on the same spot, ripped and thread-worn holes. Since I'm kneeling down trying my best to coax out this small orange kitten, I view this mess of a person from the knees down. I begin to ramble.

"Uh, hello. I'm trying to catch this kitten that ran under here. Did you happen to see where it went? I mean, I heard it crying that cat distress cry, and then, I saw it run this way. Well, I think so. You see, I remembered a very strange story that really happened so very long ago. I was shaken for sure! Have you ever had a 'déjà vu' occurrence?"

I stop talking on and on to this fragrant personage who appeared out of nowhere. I shut up. Zip my lips. Say no more. Wait for him/her/it to answer me.

My eyes travel slowly up to the face. Clearly, this is a female of indeterminate old age with a few chin whiskers curling up around her collar.

I rise slowly, shaking out my tingling legs, in response to being sat upon for such a long cat interaction, which has yet to yield any cat.

We stand eye to eye. She does not say a word. She stands as still as a guard at Buckingham Palace. She waits. I wait. No kitten.

For three long minutes that feel like an hour, we stare at each other. I itch to check my watch, knowing my lunch time is about over. I peer at her with a purpose, not willing to let her win. I have made a juvenile staring contest the most important part of my day. Our contest ends with the rustling of leaves and a kitten-sized screech—a flash of orange dashes over and around our feet.

I stoop low with both hands ready to catch the kitten. Surprisingly faster than I, the Crazy Woman bends with grace and tucks the small mewing creature into her large pocket. As if I am the one with the stinky hair and torn clothes, she makes a quick exit.

I try to protest. I try to call out, but nothing comes from my mouth. My useless feet have rooted to the ground. My mouth opens and closes like an old screen door.

Dumbfounded, I watched her speed away with the kitten I was going to rescue. When she reaches the edge of the park nearest the trees, she turns and makes eye contact once more. She's certain I'm watching her.

"Everybody lies," the Crazy Woman says, clear as day. Before I can react, she's gone.

"Tell me something I don't know, woman!" I shout into thin air.

My Vinca mind spins, but my work-self manages to recover. I sprint back to my task of problem solving, undercutting, snide remarks, and the job I love to hate. Before I stop at the crosswalk that will take me back to the office complex, I consider what happened with a smile on my face and a determination to move on.

I can hardly wait to share every detail of the story filled with cheery humor with my sister, Meadow, who is a middle school teacher. She can use a fresh story in the middle of her day. She shares the funniest ones with me. We have a friendly competition to see who can top the other. She almost always wins.

Meadow, twenty-nine, with the small, delicate features of our beautiful black mother, exudes grace. Her skin tone, rich like mom's, and her gorgeous brown eyes combine to a pleasant loveliness that matches her personality. Her six-year-old son, my one and only nephew, Caleb, resembles her so much that his dad looks like a stranger. They never married, not right for them at all, according to Meadow, but they make the living arrangements work. She and Caleb live with her best friend, Autumn, and two other teachers in a roomy old home in Summerville near the school.

Gentle in spirit but strong in character, her students know, you better not cross her. How I sometimes wish I had inherited some of her sass rather than my strange mix of our white father and black mother. I have a year-round rich tan, wavy dark hair infused with a blonde streak, and a rare birth anomaly called Poliosis, which has been my trademark. Lucky Stripe, Cruella Deville, and Skunk are just a few of many odd nicknames from my growing up. In my professional world, people will describe me as the tall woman with the strange hair. I'm almost a foot taller than Meadow with my dad's slender beanpole build. I stop to send her a quick teaser text.

'I know you are knee deep in middle school drama, but my day will beat yours! Call me when you can for all the details. For once, it is not work that wins today!' I text and resume my sprint to the glass front doors. The reflection of colorful leaves creates a glass canvas, rich and calming. Just as I run up the second flight of stairs, she pings in with, 'Thumbs up and laughing face.'

The rest of the afternoon flies by as I complete the report of the day and check on the ten people under me with my eagle eye surveillance. I try not to think too much about the crazy park event. I find my mind wandering to the red belt flash that the mom with the stroller seemed to evoke. I see that little orange tabby in the woman's pocket, and I want it for myself. I name her CW, short for Crazy Woman. I can give a cat a much better home than she can! I name him/her Rascal. Back to work, mind on fire, back to work, mind drifting, back to work, mind in a storm of fire, all on repeat for the few hours left of the day.

"Uh, V? Are you planning to leave today anytime soon?" Clacinda asks.

"What? You scared the life out of me! I didn't even see you coming. Geez, give a girl some warning next time!"

"I said, are you planning to leave anytime soon?"

"Yeah, yeah... just maybe 15 more minutes to finish this draft. Why?"

"The boss lady stopped by before you got back from lunch and told the team we need to support you more. So, she made a change in protocol. We can't leave until you leave."

"Oh." I go to my standard one-word monotone reply when I don't know what else to say. I stare at the ten sets of eyes, counting down the 15 minutes more that I have unknowingly tacked on to their day by this new team-building protocol. I let loose a sigh, ready to end this firecracker of an afternoon. I look at everyone with the best team face I can muster and say, "Give me 5 minutes, then we can all go."

They all stand and grab purses, work bags, lunch bags, and push chairs under desks. I gather my things. I close my laptop to take home so I will at least have the draft completed by the morning. They all move at once to shut down their devices and move past me with a murmured goodbye suitable for the end of an office day.

"Oh, just in case you didn't notice, we can't shut down our devices until you do. I hope you have a great evening, and maybe you will consider going in to hash this out with our Boss Lady before we have to live through this ridiculousness another day. And, just in case you need to hear it, I got your back, and I think you are a fair team manager." Clacinda's parting words are on repeat down each step and out the door as my phone buzzes. Seeing Meadow on the caller ID shifts me into Big Sis mode as I answer.

"Via, what can possibly have happened to you that will top my middle school drama?" She made Vinca into Via when she was nearly two.

"This crazy woman in the park told me Everybody Lies!" I recall the details as clearly as if I am reliving them to my spellbound sister, who laughs at my horror and sets free all the tension of the day. When I mention the red belt memory as the catalyst, she asks me, "What really happened that day? I mean, I wasn't even born yet, but you and Oakley love to tell that story over and over."

" 'I let a neighbor girl cut my beautiful hair' is mom's version of the story. Remember how she loved to sit us down at night and brush our hair 100 strokes? I hated that torture as my hair was filled with so many tangles.

"Anyway, we were friends as far as three-year-olds go. She wanted to play Salon and asked me to go first. She gave me a haircut from the scalp down, just taking a chunk out here and there, but not too much off the ends. She told me that it looked great. As I recall, she did not let me have my turn at all. When Daddy saw it, he just laughed. So I was proud that my hair must be just fine.

"But, when I walked around to show Momma my new 'do, she went crazy! She grabbed that red belt and let me have it. All the while yelling, 'How could you let that girl do this to you? Your beautiful hair is ruined!' "

We both laugh at the memory, bitter-sweet and filled with angst, rolling into my first awareness that everybody lies. Somehow, it's not so funny anymore.

"Try not to think about this too much. So your day was filled with some craziness. Sometimes I think you need something to make you laugh. What about work? How is that new client doing?"

"Oh, yeah, while I was being accosted in the park by the woman who speaks volumes with a tabby rescue, my boss mandated that my team has to support me more."

"That doesn't sound so bad!"

"Wait...she is making them stay at work as long as I do. They can't even log out of their devices until I do."

Laughing, "I am sure your mind has already figured out five ways to solve this, and all will be well in your world again. I've got to go, Via, I have a date with a handsome young man."

"You have a date? Details, please."

"Caleb's waiting on me to take him for an ice cream for our midweek treat. You can't get a better date than that! Do you want to meet us there?"

"I can't today, but I'll put it on my calendar for next week. Don't tell him that I said no today. Just let him know Auntie Via will be there next week, my treat! Love you."

"Love you, too. Bye!"

The week wore on like a bad movie script. The boss would not release her new protocol until conditions improve or one entire week passes. So, when I feel ten sets of eyes on me around 4:45 PM, I know it is time for me to stop, so they can leave. I find myself taking more and more work home.

I'm actually looking forward to ice cream with Meadow and Caleb as the one and only date in my week, not work-related. Are a six-year-old, and my sister, all the dating I can handle?

Chapter 2
Magic and Medicine

Having a standing date with my sister and my sweet nephew provides me with something to look forward to every week. Caleb was born during her second year of teaching. According to Meadow, his dad, Jonathan, is a sweet man, but "isn't a consideration for a long-term commitment." They like each other a lot, more like a best friend relationship for them both. He sees Caleb regularly, but has a life of his own. Meadow does, too. Caleb always reminds me to play well and to relax more. Awesome advice from a six-year-old has a way to humble me in just the right doses.

Meadow has mastered the perfect combination of sarcasm and tenderness required for teaching middle schoolers. When we were growing up, we lived in our imaginations. Making up games and worlds where we could regularly escape was a comfortable norm for us. I take credit for some of her teacher-training common sense from all our childhood challenges.

The red belt memory blast has our Momma close and whispering around me, to me, and yet out of reach. I can inhale, and the soapy lilac scent of clean, crisp fabric and acrid dye combines to create her trademark scent. An artist of the best kind, she was so comfortable with herself and in her own lovely dark skin. She created collages, paintings, and movement with fabric accessories. Magical and magnetic, you believed in her and you believed in her art. Her cultural elegance, deeply Gullah, wrapped itself around you, primal with beautiful tones and melodies. This made the sting of the red belt even more shocking and out of character.

She and my father met in the most unusual of ways. She entranced him from the first moment. Charles Frederick Murray, MD, a very white Baltimore native and a Hopkins grad, saw her as a patient. Of course, he remained professional and treated her with the protocol that doctor/patient relationships demand. He noticed her grace and cheekbones. She noticed his intensity and blue eyes. Unacknowledged observations put in perspective, safely ignoring and wondering at the same time.

She arrived for the last time as a patient, grateful and last-minute. He announced that he had cured her of all complaints and would see her in ten years for a follow-up. She lingered as the last patient of the day. They talked of life, disappointments, and dreams. He was captivated. She was grateful. The wondering won out over the ignoring.

She mailed a hand-painted card to thank him for taking such good care of her. She wished him well and wrote that the two of them would see better days. After mulling that over, by reading into the line "the two of us" some hidden innuendo, he mustered up the courage to call her. They could not see each other until the patient/doctor relationship was completely severed. Email and phone calls provided a safe distance for them to learn about each other with only words between them.

Dad fired her as a patient after sending a request to the AMA. Two years later, thriving in the culture and art of the city, they were married. He called her Angel. She called him Charlie. She kept her professional name that she worked so hard to establish.

We called her Momma. Christened Annalise Rosemay Pringle, she grew up in Adams Run, South Carolina, a dot on the map on the way to Edisto Island near Charleston. Live oaks older than the generations they shade, draped with Spanish moss hung like silken hair, covered the landscape.

The black community speaks the language of Gullah. Momma and her art left this land and moved to Baltimore for college, culture, and a way to be appreciated for who she was. Falling in love with a white doctor was not part of her perfect plan.

My brother, Oakley, who is the middle child of the three of us, looks exactly like our white dad. He and I were born in Baltimore. When Momma's kinfolk all died off, they left her the house she grew up in. Daddy moved us south, filled with dread of the Southern way, with his beautiful black wife and two mixed children. He started practicing medicine at the nearest hospital's outpatient clinic.

They navigated enrolling us in proper public schools. Mrs. Pringle taught art at the High School of Summerville, and that allowed us to attend school across district lines as a teacher perk. She loved her job. We loved the ride into and from home, singing loudly to the radio, laughing about her students, and her day.

Soon, Meadow was on the way, the only one of us born in the Lowcountry looking like our Momma born again.

No children could have grown up freer and more restricted at the same time. Momma made magic, and Daddy started drinking.

Chapter 3
Just Slow

One of the biggest conundrums of the Lowcountry is the speed at which we move. Slow. Just slow. Slow to change. Slow to adapt. Slow to rush you out of a conversation. Our infrastructure has not kept up with our growth. There are only so many roads to create when you're surrounded by rivers that converge into the ocean. So, the horrendous traffic sets the tone for the day.

After a time of deep and abiding loss, I found my condo. The need for something that I own myself, true and free, provides stability. I live in a sweet community of older settled people who like to host suppers, play games, have Happy Hours in the green space, and look after each other. It's off the beaten path just enough to feel like I live on the land, but close enough to my office that I can usually drive there in thirty minutes. With three bedrooms, an open living space and kitchen, a screened back porch, and a lovely soaker tub, Georgie, my calico, and I take the owner's bedroom, with one guest room and one work-at-home office space. I selected calm colors for the walls and flooring in naturals, grays, blues, and tans.

Meadow added color with pillows, accent chairs, photographs, and Caleb's artwork to the rooms. I can sit on my porch and sip my tea with Georgie. To see my place, you would assume that I live a contented life, and you would be right. For the most part, that is. My job, my memories, my mistakes can jab and push at my sore spots, especially the ones that I avoid, ignore, and deny.

I move slowly and gently through the evening. More than ready to put this day behind me, I settle into my bed with a good book and good company as the weight of Georgie sneaking onto my bed makes me laugh every time.

"Look, Missy, you are more than welcome in here. You do not have to hide. Yes, you are a beautiful cat. Hey, you almost got a sibling today. I tried my best to rescue this adorable kitten. Now, just know it was not more lovely than you."

She answers with purrs and pats my cheek with her paw, falling into a peaceful sleep.

We both startle awake from my alarm. Another day in the office awaits as I shower, dress, feed us both, and leave in plenty of time to get ahead of the traffic. I make office plans all the way to work.

I drive into work, navigating the normal traffic tie-ups with experience. I leave extra early for the day with at least an hour to myself. Once Charleston was selected as the number one place to live several years in a row, the people longing for the coast moved here in vast numbers to our small stretch of land.

When I am highly stressed, I do something. I destress by cleaning out a closet or organizing a room, making a ten-step plan to solve a problem. All things that make me very well oriented for my job. The stop-and-go traffic depletes all of my extra early bird solitude. By the time I pull into the parking lot, I've decided, amended, added, and detracted several versions of Plan A.

I close the door of my fire engine red SUV, taking a deep breath of the fresh fall air, appreciating the blue-tinted sky. The fluttering butterflies shimmer on the blooms of the lantana planted on each side of the building's glass doors. I raise my coffee mug, taking the steps to my office with determination. Here's to the last day of ten pairs of eyes waiting for me to leave so they can.

"Good morning, team! Let's all rejoice that this will be the last day you are forced to stay until I leave," I begin.

Shouts of positive responses circle the room, and then laughter. I see a slight improvement in the sincere smiles as I look at each team member. I glance at Clacinda. I cannot tell you what made me linger on her for longer than the others. I see her differently today. Something is off, but I can't figure out what.

"Clacinda, will you stop by my desk?"

"Uh, now?"

"Yes, now."

As she makes her way to my desk, I watch her sigh, sniff, throw her shoulders back, and make herself taller.

"Are you okay?"

"Of course!"

"Something seems off today."

"Nothing I can't handle, right? You know how we just do what we have to do? Well, that is my mantra and where I am today. You probably felt some of that vibe from me. No worries. I will get my share of the work done. Not a problem."

"This isn't about the share of the work! It's about you. I'll take you at your word. As your team leader, I want to be sure you're okay."

She smiles a half smile and turns to walk back to her desk.

"I'm good. You're good. It's all good." She throws lies over her shoulder.

This is the first conversation I've had with any of the team members that possibly touched on their lives outside of this job. How sad is that?

I pull my laptop out and prepare my desk to start the daily tasks, distracted and unfocused. My eyes rest on the open laptop, but my mind begins to wander.

The laptop sits open on the desk of the extended stay hotel, logged in to the virtual school classroom assignment page. The baby cries. The two-year-old

joins in. A chorus of high-pitched noise enters the student's brain, settling into the core where the instinct to scream, "Make it stop!" lives.

"Shhh. I got this," her brother assures her as he picks up the crying baby and soothes the two-year-old. Another cycle of chaos unfolds.

The older siblings care for the babies in an extended stay hotel, the only workable plan for a mother evicted, newly employed, and hopeless. She assigns the older siblings two hours each on the open laptop. The assignment page relentlessly calls to them as they try to do what their mother has asked of them. They cycle through, one in charge of the babies, one in school for two-hour shifts, from 8 AM to 5 PM. School and child care. A home of sorts, as their mother works to save enough for a deposit on a rental that could be home again.

The room phone rings, startling the almost-asleep baby into the high-pitched wailing once again. The sister rocks this time. Silent tears plop onto the laptop as she takes the phone off the hook.

The knock at the door is more insistent. "Never open this door when I am not here!" echoes around the room. The open laptop, and the four siblings try to disappear. Everybody lies.

I jump up from the desk so quickly, my ergonomic chair slides back two feet, hitting the soothing shade of gray wall.

"Sorry, sorry! Gotta go. Too much coffee!" I say over my shoulder to the room of startled teammates.

I can't. I just can't explain anymore that vision and all it evokes in me. All the other vivid visions have been my family, my history. This one is not any of that, and yet, something about it is eerily familiar. I rush out of the office and into the chrome and mirrors restroom. That voice. Those words. Those kids.

"You are fine. Really, get a grip, Vinca!" I tell myself, patting my face with a wet paper towel, running my fingers through my hair. A few deep cleaning breaths settle my nerves a bit.

Another moment and I have regained my composure enough to walk back out and act normal, at least normal for me. I can't focus on this, or my day is ruined. I shift my focus with the purpose of guiding the small business owner/client with an action plan for expanding the market of her natural lotions and soaps.

That is where my focus is needed. That is where I will direct my mind to go. Still, that laptop, those kids, that voice, follow me, as real as the teammates in my office space.

Instead of going back to work, I sent a quick memo to my team.

'Ladies, something came up. I'll be back after lunch.'

The line of shops on the Town Square in this quaint downtown is varied. They have been transformed into many lives over time. From our local talent theater with the billboard placards and hand-lettered marquee to eclectic food options from tapas to a coffee shop and wine bar, our main street offers as much for the visitor as well as the local. Two of my favorite stops are the small-front, deep-back book store and our local pharmacy. Where else can you select books from local authors as well as best sellers and get tips and pointers from the staff picks? Where else can you get a hand-scooped serving of ice cream along with your prescription needs?

Soaking in the cooler air, I detour through the scarecrows displayed along the center of the town square. The displays put together by local groups to represent their theme draw people of all ages to stop and enjoy the art. My mom loved this tradition and put together fabulous displays of color and shapes, each year, better than the one before. I swallow back a lump in my throat that came out of nowhere, remembering her theme of harvest with a life-sized cornucopia that we helped her set up. Sharp and intense, missing hits my core for my mom and her art, for the love and creativity she added to everything. An ice cream would really make my day.

When my parents moved to Adams Run, Momma thrived in so many ways. We lived our lives in between the tides, near the ocean and marsh-filled rivers, eating the shrimp we caught, so sweet and delicious. She taught as if she were called to teach. Her spirit was strong, and she insisted we grow up believing in something so much more than ourselves.

On silent feet, the cancer moved into her ovaries and took over her body so rapidly that when she was diagnosed, the time to treat and recover was simply gone. We succumbed to her rapidly declining existence. Freeing her soul from her decimated body provided us relief and joy as we listened to her last breath.

I watch as the cashier bags various small items for the customer before me.

"Here you go, Mr. Williams. In a small bag, just like you asked for!" He hands his customer the purchase.

Not again. What is happening to me?

The brown paper bag, the perfect size for one can of beer, sits folded in half and half again creased with the edge of a fingernail and put into a front shirt pocket. Daddy leaves the house at 7 PM, after supper and the news, taking the bag with him to his best friend's store. A small offering of a bit of everything from slices of bologna to cold beer in red, white, and blue cans that fit perfectly, hidden in that unfolded paper bag. Daddy drank one beer in the store with Mr. Mack. He listens well, laughs at all the same old stories and jokes. He shoots the breeze with elegance and trust that only a best friend can offer. One more can in the bag for the ride home, adding a bag of peanuts for us children. A sad white man attending a black Home Going Celebration for the first time in his life slips a folded paper bag creased with a finger nail into the casket of his best friend.

"Everybody lies."

"Miss, how can I help you?" The cashier's question breaks through another family vision. I realize this is at least the second time I've been asked.

"Ineedicecream," I answer. She laughs.

"Mint-Chocolate-Chip. One scoop," I manage a minuscule smile back, attempting to enter the real world once again with cone in hand.

I'm losing the last bit of sanity I have worked so hard to maintain. My heart beats in a steady, rapid pace. My breathing becomes shallower. I savor every bite of my treat.

Looking over my shoulder, across the square, and back around, I fully expect to see the CW and the kitten from last week following me. I don't know which is worse, her voice in my head or her presence in my path. All these out-of-body experiences, like I am a fly on the wall of some bizarre time machine. I see, smell, hear, and fully experience the vision. No sign of her anywhere. I pick up my pace and head toward the park where I first saw them last week.

I look for the mom with the baby stroller, thinking she comes here often, and I can ask her about the woman and the kitten. No sign of them. I walk to the bench and sit for a minute to calm myself down. With my head tilted back, I let the autumn sun do its magic, gently entering through my pores and filling me with the sun's vitamins.

The leaves rustle, and a short mew breaks into my space. My eyes snap open in time to see the tabby flash by. I jump up, sure that I know the way this time to the tree with the huge root system. Before the kitten dashes under the roots, I scoop it up. Hissing and mewing louder and louder, I try to convince it that my intentions are good.

"Okay, you little sneak. No need to worry! I am the safest human you can possibly meet." I scratch behind its ears and speak cat talk in a calm, gentle manner. As the mewing turns to purring, I catch the sour hair odor. The CW is near. She stares ahead. She's waiting on me to make the next move. When my little friend sees her, it wriggles out of my hand and runs to her, swirling its body between her feet, around, and back again. She still just stares. Maybe she's having a stroke?

"Hello. Are you okay?" She doesn't appear to hear me or to be able to respond.

"Ugh, I saw you last week. Remember? Is this your cat?"

Nothing but that same blank expression. She carefully catches the kitten and places it in her pocket. Before she turns away and begins to walk into the edge of the trees, her soft voice states, "Everybody lies."

So frustrated and filled with memories, tender and bittersweet, I turn on my heels and rush back toward the office. Once again mystified and confused, I take a detour, pull out my phone, and text my baby brother, Oakley.

'Can you talk?'

'Yeah, what's up?'

I call him. Usually we resolve any cares of the day by texting. Today, I have such a jumble of thoughts that would lose translation in a text barrage. He has a wicked sense of humor, and I can always use a good laugh, even if it is at myself.

I have not filled him in about my life's ups and downs in a while. He's a voice of reason and a book of advice I can open whenever I need a good talking to or a calming perspective. He, of the three of us, is the steady one. He's also the only one of us who can live with Dad and keep all of his brain cells alive and running. He answers right away.

"Hey, Big Sis, what's up with you? Are you okay?"

"Yes. I mean, for the most part, yes, but strange things have been happening. I need to hear a voice of reason along with my weekly 'sympathy for my single sister' ice cream date with Meadow and Caleb. You know what I mean?"

"Sure, but that actually doesn't sound half bad to me!"

"I have a lot going on at work, as usual. I've come to realize how many times people in my life coat the truth with so many layers of lies. First, it was just family stuff, like deeply buried memories that were triggered by something I saw or sensed. Now, one of my coworkers has joined in. I seem to have made myself an unofficial seeker of the truth just so I can be right or say I told you so! Like, I am Superwoman for catching someone lying."

"Sounds like your normal manner of managing life to me..."

We both laugh. I feel my anxiety lessening already.

"Anyway, last week, I decided to have my lunch in Azalea Park. You know, fresh air and all that. I saw a young mom with a toddler, and she had on a red belt. I entered this weird flashback mode of mom reacting to the neighbor girl's haircut episode that cost me a spanking and half of my hair. Next, I heard a kitten. An orange tabby-the little thing like flashes by me. Of course, I follow it..."

I chatter on and on, retelling him the episode where I first encountered the woman, the office flashbacks, and the woman and kitten a second time. He listens, interjecting his comments at just the right times and making me laugh over and over.

"Sis, I think these are all just strange coincidences. Though I admit, a woman saying the same thing you are wondering is very weird. Go on back inside and finish your day. Drive out to the house and have dinner with Dad and me. I have some fresh shrimp, and I can add some grits to the menu. We can eat like Lowcountry natives, sit out on the porch, and shoot the breeze."

"I don't know. How is Dad today? It's hard to see him less than his normal self. I'm a coward and a failure of a daughter. You and Meadow are both so much better with him than I am."

"While some of that may be true, come on out anyway. In fact, pack an overnight bag and stay with us. Bring Georgie, too. We can take my johnboat out at sunrise and relax, catch a few fish. He would love to see you!"

"I don't know. Let me finish the afternoon, and I'll get back to you! I'm saying yes to dinner. You already have my stomach growling for your shrimp and grits. I'll text you before I leave here. Okay, thank you. Just... well, thank you."

"You need a break, that's all I'm saying. See you soon!"

Just like that, my day takes a turn for the better. I ease back into the building, climb the stairs, and slip in behind my desk. I open my laptop, answer emails with the efficiency of a professional.

Occasionally, I scan the room to see if my team is on task or acting like they are on task. For the most part, everyone looks like they are trying to finish work so they can leave when the time comes. We do have a work policy that states you can set your own hours. As long as the work is done to a high standard, you can leave for the day or a vacation. We even encourage the team to take mental health days off. That is why this new directive of staying as long as I stay has hit us so hard. I really do love so many parts of this job. I really do want to trust people. The struggle is real.

Maybe Oakley is right about needing a break. I think I will pack an overnight bag and stay with him and Dad. It has been so long since I went fishing. The Lowcountry river system winds and narrows, widens and pulses through the edge of spartina grass held together with pluff mud, oysters, and fiddler crabs. Pungent and sharp, the nose cringes when a breath of air laced with the oily mud hits the senses. It's the scent of home laced with memory that never gets old.

The early morning river, calm and still, wakes from the boat, slicing a perfect V along the surface as we putter to our secret fishing hole. Great herons startle and rise, expanding their wings like angels lifting off to circle and land with a splash. A fish breaks the surface of the water and glides airborne for a few feet, so we know they are waiting for us to drop our lines.

Sometimes, we keep a few; mostly, we catch and release. All of us Murrays can catch bait, put it on the line, and cast with a graceful ease taught by our Grand Pap on our Momma's side. His beautiful brown skin glistening in the sun, his smile of pride creased around his mouth,

26

revealing his straight white teeth so perfect and strong. Our white doctor daddy never did master the art of fishing like his children did, but he's always willing to try one more time. When we acclimated to Adams Run and living in the house we came to visit every spring and holiday growing up, we discovered a deep love of this place where our Momma grew up.

'Yes, I will pack a bag and fish with you in the morning. I let Georgie know she will be eating fish this weekend. That cat loves fish! You are right, Baby Brother, I need this break. Should be there in an hour or so, considering the traffic.'

He replies with a 'heart'. How can so many lies be covered with one heart?

Chapter 4
The Golden Hour

I drive the route to my family home with autopilot surety. I know every pothole in the road intimately. The turns and slowdowns, the up to highway speed, and the lovely oaks that line the highway are old friends. The most enchanting time is the golden hour when the sunlight sends intense beams between the limbs of the oaks, producing a strobe light show that causes drivers to reach for their shades in defense. This particular light hits the side of your vision where those glasses are useless. The only defense is your hand on the window, making a temporary visor to keep you from the hypnotic light show's power. The sky deepens to a violet hue laced with orange where the clouds bounce back, and the Lowcountry really shows off. Photos taken in this light are magical. What has taken me so long to drive out here?

I turn up the music. Turn off the AC. Let down the windows, belting out a song like I'm on stage, in a chorus line, or on a music award show that discovers my true talent. I sing like this every time I travel this road, remembering and forgetting all twined together. Home. Home again. Home away from home.

I face my return home as my tires crunch on the looping gravel drive. I ease into the paved area in front of the garage my dad added to the property when we moved here for good. He used to have a running list of improvements he thought my grandparents should make to the old house. Fortunately, he was able to accomplish a lot of them before

Momma got too sick and he got too drunk. Now, Oakley takes on the rest of dad's list, one repair at a time, around and between his work responsibilities and dad's medical needs.

"Well, look what the cat drug in! Oakley, she's here! Flower Bud, I am so glad to see you! And even that spoiled rotten Georgie feline."

"Oh, Daddy!" I open my arms to hug him around his walker frame, trying to manage the delicate balance between just right to satisfy us both and not enough to wound his pride by making him lose his balance. He can't see my eyes tear as the reality of his thin, birdlike frame hits me in the heart.

"Oakley's been in the kitchen all afternoon, and it smells like the best 5-star place in New York City. Come on in! Let's sit on the porch until he calls us. You can catch me up on your life."

Well, there's the tightrope walk I traverse. What he really wants is for me to tell him that I have met someone and am dating said someone worthy of me, so he can stop wondering what will become of his Flower Bud. I don't discuss my nonexistent love life with him. After too many bad, heart-wrenching breakups, it's best just to let that be a topic we avoid. My mind warms up to the latest problem at work, and I decide I will go that route with a little Meadow and Caleb mixed in. I should be safe until dinner.

He rolls his walker up the newly installed ramp and settles easily into his favorite wide wicker chair. The deep cushions in shades of blue and white that Momma picked out mold themselves around him. He sits with a soft sigh. The glass of chipped ice glistens in the setting sunlight as condensation slips down his ever-present scotch and water. His hand trembles as he reaches for the drink. He takes a two-handed approach to bring it to his lips. Georgie has already made herself at home in the chair across from him.

"What's your poison? The usual?"

"That'll do just fine," I answer and slide back on the porch swing.

"Oakley, bring Big Sis a glass of that wine!"

I relax into the wooden slatted swing just in time to inhale the sunset in all its glory. I push off with my toes and lift my legs, curling them under me. I gently sway and listen to my dad, mumble my replies, and relax. Only stopping to hug Oakley as he brings my wine and tells us dinner is in thirty minutes.

We move inside before the mosquitoes can light and make our way through the front room to the screened porch. Daddy expanded this porch so that we could have a dining area as well as an art studio for Momma. She could be protected from the elements, but still feel as if she were outside as she created and planned. He and Oakley have not changed much. This room holds our hearts.

My brother set the table with cloth napkins, place mats, and a vase of tea olive clippings emitting the heady scent of fresh, clean air. As we sat around the table, we laughed more than we ate. The familiar sound of flatware on pottery scooping up the creamy grits mixes with the delicate shrimp perched on top is easy on our palates. He even made the kind of biscuits that easily split open, revealing the flaky centers.

I've missed this place as much as I've missed these two! The dinner over and our chairs pushed back, we talk, much as we did our whole lives, over the end of the meal and before the clean up. Sweet in-between time where we have no limit to protect or allow a revealing of sorts. My family.

"Daddy, when you first explained to me how we were given our most unusual nature names, I was so embarrassed. I mean, who names all three of their children after a flower, a tree, and a land form? But you said, Momma insisted on picking the names that represented the people we would grow into being. All I could think of was how people stared at the five of us everywhere we went. You, white as you can be. Momma, black as she could be. Me, a mix of both with my blonde stripe, Oakley white like you, and Meadow black like Momma. Adding our unusual names to that was just a lot for my younger self. Now, though, I see Momma had vision. I like that she was unafraid to blaze trails."

"I still miss her every day. Everyday. From the time I really saw her, I was changed," his voice catches. He takes his time to compose himself. "I hope you three always know you were raised by a fierce woman who loved more than anyone I know."

"Here's to Momma!" We raise our glasses and touch them together in a salute to this Sea Island Lowcountry woman who wove us together into a family of many hues and shades of the same skin covering us all.

After a quiet evening, I sleep in my teenage bedroom I shared with Meadow, and let out a deep sigh. Sounds of Oakley and Dad's bedtime routine fall on my ears. Meds dispensed. Feet shuffling as the walker slides upon the heart of pine original floors of the house. Chuckles and good-natured nudges between father and son drift in and out. A wave of love for my brother washes over me. He's taking far better care of our dad than I could have ever imagined. His mobility issues gradually increased with each setback. From a lifetime of smoking, drinking to forget, and the high stress of an on-call physician, his health declined rapidly. The three of us had to have our frank discussions of how to manage Dad's care.

"There is no discussion. Period," Oakley began. "I am the child who'll be the caregiver for our Dad. You and Meadow have too much to work around. I can work my own hours from wherever I am. I can lift him and drive him to appointments. I need to do this more than I can say. End of discussion."

We just hugged and cried and moved him in. What a depth of gratitude I have for my brother!

I have my alarm set for the sunrise fishing, a creek to river run, which we planned out earlier this evening. I know I won't need it as I settle into the bed with the squeaks still in all the same places. My eyes close with a smile on my face that only comes from contentment. Georgie curls beside me. Her purrs set the peaceful tone like a lullaby.

Chapter 5
Something's Gotta Kill Me

I wake up in the utter darkness and check the time. Perfect. I can make myself some coffee and walk out to the old weathered wooden dock where our johnboat is waiting. I pull on my leggings and t-shirt, grab my roomy hoodie, and tiptoe toward the kitchen. As I turn the corner, I see the light on and Oakley sipping his coffee, scrolling through his phone. Georgie lets me know she is happy to have her breakfast too.

"You're just in time!"

"I planned on having coffee ready for you, but I should've known you were on this! Are you sure Daddy will be okay while we fish? Funny how being here makes me revert back to calling him Daddy."

"Yeah, he often sleeps in, and I go out on my own to see what I can catch for us. He knows how to text me or call from his phone, and we have a neighbor down the way who could get here before me if needed. One thing we decided when we made this arrangement was that I needed to be able to live my life too, have some free time. He would be looked after, or we would make arrangements. It may not be perfect, but it has worked well so far. Drink up, or put yours in a to-go container. I'm ready to roll!"

Laughing, I pour my coffee with a splash of half and half, add one more for good measure, into one of the assorted containers left over from who knows when. This one is painted with a huge sunflower, no doubt one of Momma's touches. This makes me feel like I am taking her along with us.

We help each other launch the boat like a choreographed ballet duet. We know our parts without even talking. We putter along in the still waters of the morning. Pulling up our hoodies for mosquito protection, we follow the bends and turns of the river as the sky lightens from navy blue to orange. We turn east and pause long enough to watch the sun edge over the horizon, sipping our brews, breathing in the salt-laced air, and thanking God for his creation. Once the sun crests, we can begin the serious fishing.

"I'm taking you to my secret, I mean top-secret like National Security Breach, secret fishing hole. In other words, you can't tell anyone where this is. I can blindfold you, or you can swear on your lifelong happiness that you will not divulge this to anyone, even on threat of torture. Which do you choose?"

"Really? Come on, first of all, who would I tell? Secondly, no one I know could actually find this place, and thirdly, of course, I swear not to reveal your big secret. If you remember, I kept lots of your confessions, admissions, and mistakes locked away for all of our lives like a good Big Sis does, right?"

"In that case, I'm certain we will not only catch fish, we'll stock the freezer for the next time you come. You need to persuade Meadow and Caleb to come too!"

"Deal!"

He steers the boat with ease, and I sit back letting my hair fly in the wind, watching the small wake rippling on the water as we glide down and around all the twists and turns of a salt marsh ecosystem. I didn't know how badly I needed this until I am here now. Letting all the stress of my job, the weird woman, the kitten, and the fact that everybody lies go, I drift in and out, rocked by the rhythm of the boat, into a lazy lull of peace.

"Hey, grab the anchor, V!" Oakley brings me back to reality.

"Over here?" He nods. I toss the anchor into the water at the back of the boat and feel it catch. We settle into a routine of two people who have fished together a lot. Knowing how to cast, where to move around the other person, and how to be quiet, we cast and reel in over and over. We're not in any great hurry. We're not getting any hits, not even a nibble.

"Looks like the freezer will be pretty empty from this trip!"

"Yeah, nothing's biting today except those mosquitoes when we set out. Are you willing to try a little longer before we head back, say thirty more minutes?"

"Sure, it's nice to have this time without thinking Daddy will overhear us. How is he really doing?"

"What you see is what you get. He was on his best behavior for you last night. He's a mix between what he's supposed to do, what he knows he's supposed to do, and what he actually does. He keeps repeating 'something's gotta kill me one day' every time he lights up or takes his evening beverage, starting at midday. Overall, he's okay. High risk for so many problems in the future."

"I figured as much. How do you put up with his lack of compliance? I'd be so angry all the time."

"Well, I'm in a virtual support group, which helps. But mostly, I'm determined to let him live out the rest of his life on his terms, however long or short that ends up being. I can't make him do anything he doesn't want to do."

"He's not been the same since we lost Momma. He looks thinner and more feeble since I was last here."

"Well, I can still lift him onto the johnboat and ride him up and down the creek. He won't fish. Feels too unstable when he tries to cast and too weak when I cast for him. Learned that the hard way, but we have had some great sunset rides watching the porpoises dip and dance right beside us. There's life left in him, V. I'm not certain how much, but it is there.

"What about you? When you called, and I talked you into all this fun, you sounded so confused and stressed. What's going on with you?"

I told him all the bizarre events, mixing in my own slant on it, much like the ever storyteller entertaining my siblings when our Momma was creating and our Daddy on a call or a binge.

We laughed so hard at the smell of the Crazy Woman, the tricky antics of the kitten, and the whole mess of everybody lies. This is what I think as we pull anchor, fish-less and satiated with the salt marsh life teeming around us. I made a humorous tale of a serious coincidence of my biggest pet peeve and societal downfall.

Yes, indeed, everybody lies.

After we tie up the boat and listen to Daddy harass us for no fish, I load up the car with a care package of leftovers and start back inland, driving myself and Georgie cat back to reality.

Our visit conversation runs through my head like the winding creek I grew up loving. I think back to the tests and twists of our lives, my two siblings and I, rushing about in play. I grab my heart space, remembering the eyes of the strangers that seared into us, trying to figure out our back story. My slim white father and my small boned black mother walk into a room with their offspring. My lovely mix of the two of them, complete with the blonde streak, laughing at something funny my white brother said, hand in hand with my black sister, in all our radiance. Sometimes, a stranger would ask if we were adopted. If they but looked carefully, they would see the father/son resemblance, the mother/daughter similarities, and me with the features of both strong and true to the DNA. We all handled it well.

Even in the Deep South, change can be more accepted, and people can move forward instead of staying mired in the past. The younger our judges, the more tolerant they were of the glaring differences. The older folks, native and relocated, can still make the snide remark, the stare held just a bit too long. The jeers and laughing head shakes are unacknowledged by us. Our parents were our protectors and stellar teachers in the art of how to handle who you are and where you come from.

I spent the rest of the weekend relaxing on my condo's screened porch with Georgie. She loves to sit in the sun and take the best catnap ever. I watch her pink nose twitch as she sleeps, and the orange tabby enters my mind. I'm glad I told Oakley all about my experiences with The CW and her pitiful kitten. I wonder where they live. I hate to assume homelessness. I can see and even more smell that she's not taking care of herself as well as she should be. I can hear her voice with the clarity that defies all the rest of her unkempt bearing, speaking the truth, "Everybody lies."

In my family, there is a line that we never cross between what is true and what we make true. We three siblings like to say we had a happy childhood. I see that as the first lie I recognized. It took me to my knees. What is true? What do I make true to protect us? What do I believe? If our childhood was not happy, what was it?

The feeling starts as a tingle somewhere in my gut. It runs through my blood like a Tsunami of deep sadness. Everything has changed. I hate this feeling, so heavy and intrusive that it weighs on my soul. Yes, it was happy. Sure it was. We had lots of free time. We could create our own worlds. Yes!

No, our free time existed because our daddy was not there, or he was too intoxicated to care for us. Our mom was in her artist mind, and I was not to disturb her, no matter what. I, the oldest child, took care of everyone as I fed them, played with them, and made sure they were safe. Everybody lies.

Chapter 6
Collision Course of Confusion

I shake my head as if that will clear the haze of memory away. I walk around the house cleaning here and there as if putting order will release all of this. I pick up my phone to text Meadow and put it down. How can I ruin my sister's perception of our childhood with all of this that I can't explain?

I'm going to the office and get a head start on next week's tasks. That will for sure change my mindset and push me over this feeling of dread.

I drive along the route to the park. The dark feelings swirl and settle all around me like a mantle I can't shake. I check my rearview mirror and see a blue light flashing. I look for a spot to move over so that the police car can pass. What the heck? This can't be happening. I'm the person being stopped. I've never gotten a ticket in my life. I'm called Miss Rule Follower. I know I'm driving the speed limit.

I pull into a parking lot, and the squad car follows. With hands shaking, I open the glove compartment of my car and pull out the registration along with my ID. The officer makes his way to my car. He's young with a military build, and looks like he is filling his quota of traffic stops for the day with me. The feelings I haven't been dealing with threaten to push me over the edge. I will myself to shut up and listen to what he has to say.

"Driver's license and registration, Miss. I'm sure you know why I pulled you over."

"No, no, I do not know! I've never been pulled over in all my years of driving! I can't imagine what I did. I drive like a church grandma!"

"No, you don't. You failed to signal when you changed lanes."

"I disagree. I never fail to signal! I know I signaled. You must be confusing me with someone else."

The awful throat lump right before the tears come manifests itself in my anger over being falsely accused. My voice rises in pitch, a falsetto of shame screeching out.

"Wait here while I input the information and fill out your ticket." Young Policeman walks back to his cruiser with the blue light still flashing and leaves me to stew. In my state of mind, I have an out-of-body experience. I watch myself. I hear myself. I see myself as if I were a fly on the windshield.

"'Wait here while I write you a ticket!'" I say out loud in the worst middle school mocking voice.

"That arrogant little shit! Who does he think he is?" I pound my fist on the steering wheel in anger.

"I can't believe this is happen-i-n-g ..." As the tears I have tried to stuff come out in angry sobs like a three-year-old who doesn't get her way. Fifteen minutes pass as I wait and run through all these scenarios over and over again. Anger. Indignation. Self-pity. Add themselves up as Officer Tough saunters back to my car.

"Here you go. You can come to traffic court on the date indicated and give your story, or you can pay the fine." He hands me the ticket and sees my face for the first time.

"You seem very upset over this."

"Yes, that's the truth! Because you have made a mistake! I do not deserve this ticket!" I hard-cry once again. The little fly version of me on the windshield shakes its head. I am cried-out in a matter of minutes.

"Are you safe and calm enough to drive? Is there someone I can call to come and pick you up?"

"Yes, I am safe to drive. No, I am not calm. I don't deserve this ticket!"

I see another police car pull in, and Officer Tough walks over to consult what to do with hysterical me, short of tearing up the ticket. At that point, I pull myself together as they both walk up to my window.

"Look, I was upset before this happened and was going to the office to work on some projects to clear my mind. I'm going to stick with that plan as accomplishing a task always settles me. I'm even more upset now, but I am capable of excellent driving as my stellar driving history shows. I'm rolling up this window and pulling out. I'll see you in court." I say in my normal businesswoman's voice when motivating my team to focus and cut to the chase.

"That works for us," Officer Back up replies. I lip-read the last words as the window closes, and I start up my car. All the way to the office, I seethe. I need to calm myself. I need to get some control.

I park in the empty lot and walk around the car. The wind picks up, and my hair ruffles around my face. I decide to walk around to the town square and leave the work to itself. Another lovely day with the colors of fall on the scarecrows still, I walk with a purpose to the park. All the way there, I realize I am looking for the CW and her kitten. Maybe she lives nearby. Maybe she hangs out in one of the alleyways.

I sit down hard on the closest bench, barely aware of the sunlight on the leaves, the cool air around me, and the people strolling through the park. I pull out my phone to text Meadow.

'You will never believe what just happened to me!'

'You really should stop making that the first line of your texts.'

'Yeah, well, this time you will reply in all caps. I just got pulled over for not using my turn signal when changing lanes!'

'YOU?'

'See!'

'The most important part of this is, are you guilty?'

'Of course not! The cop was this young new policeman, all cocky and self-assured. He wouldn't even listen to me when I told him I had never gotten a ticket in my life! Can I call you? I can't text all the details and leave out my tone of voice.'

'Give me 5 minutes.'

I put my phone on the bench beside me and try to calm myself down. I hate, absolutely hate, to be accused of something I did not do. That ranks second only to hating lies. I know my driving instincts. I always signal. That cop and his arrogant swagger, his condescending tone, his 'let me slow down and explain to the little lady way' of speaking about traffic laws and such, infuriates me. He reminds me of my first real love. Oh, my soul...that's it! No wonder I freaked out. My phone buzzes as Meadow's picture pops up in all her beauty with Caleb's face next to hers. I smile as I pick up where I left off and give her all the details.

"Anyway, do you think your resource officer, what is his name again? Todd? Tony? Didn't you go out with him a few times?"

"Tony, and, yes, I did."

" ...so would he look at my ticket and advise me as how to take this to court? Because, I tell you, I'm not willing to pay a fine for something I didn't do!"

"Take a picture of it and text it to me. I will send it to him and see what he says. He's a good guy and will be straight with you. Honestly, Via, this is not a big deal. I mean, we all screw up sometimes, and well, this may be a first for you, but nobody's perfect. Not even you!"

"Meadow, I called you for help, not analysis! I've had the craziest experience, and I don't need your teacher talk advice right now. Just send him the photo and let me know what Todd, I mean Tony, says!"

"Excuse me for trying to help you. Maybe you need to look at this with a sense of humor. I think it is kind of funny. You may have been his first ticket of his career, and he was pulling out all stops to be sure you remain an upstanding citizen."

"Maybe in five years, I'll look back on this and laugh, but not today. Look, I've got to go. Thank you for all your help."

"Wait, how are Dad and Oakley? How was your visit?"

"Oh, Meadow, Daddy looks rough. Oakley does a great job with him and all his many needs. He and I went sunrise fishing in the johnboat, and it was great. Didn't catch a thing. Being on the water in the salt marsh never grows old. They made me promise to bring you and Caleb next time, and next time needs to be within the next month."

"That actually sounds like a good plan. Hard to see Daddy so frail, but no more excuses for me. What if we had a Thanksgiving time together? Maybe the weekend before, as soon as we get out of school? I already made plans to spend Thanksgiving with Jonathan's family so Caleb can keep connecting with that side of the family, too."

"Will Jonathan be there too?"

"I hope so for Caleb. But if not, his Aunties, cousins, and Grandparents'll be there."

"Let's do this! Listen, sorry for all the anger earlier. I'm going to try and figure out what is up with me, but you didn't deserve angry Vinca. I'll talk to Oakley and we'll make some plans. Love you, Baby Sis!"

"Yeah, yeah, - same here."

I pull the ticket from my bag and take a quick photo to send to Meadow. The faster we get this done, the better. I take one last look around the park and head back to the office.

I cross the street and walk as fast as I can, trying to burn off some of the anger with each step. Before I reach the office door, a small ball of orange fire flashes by in the form of the kitten. I stop short and watch as the CW walks out from the alleyway. Slowly and deliberately, she turns her head and stares at me. Those icy eyes set in that crepe paper face, so feral and intense, are directly in conflict with her feeble body and lumbering gait, drawing me in. I stare back until I am distracted once again by the kitten running full on across the sidewalk. I turn to see if she is going to catch my little orange buddy and place it in her pocket once again. As if she just vanished into thin air, as if I imagined her all along, no one is there. Even the cat has disappeared.

I quickly unlock the glass doors, rush in, shut them, and lock myself inside in under a minute. I run to the stairwell and sprint up to the second floor, hurry to my familiar chair and plop down, heart racing. What I know and what I think I know are on a collision course of confusion. What I believe to be true and what is actually true are so muddied into one foregone conclusion. Everybody lies.

Chapter 7
Distracted Plans and Distorted Thinking

I managed to work on the Solution Proposal Plan outline for the week with little or no distractions. The sunlight hits the office space right above my desk. I breathe in day-old coffee with a hint of cinnamon remnants from our team treats. Completing the work calms my spirit. A slow smile moves across my face. I'm in control. But, there's me in denial mode, where I am fine. You are fine. We are all just fine.

I glance at the stark white-faced clock, and I can read it at a glance. We all face the numberless time-keeper for motivation and to stay on task. Today, I decide that time's up. Anticipating my porch and my feline, I lock up. My feet tap and echo a quick beat of retreat. Nothing out of the ordinary happens as I start up my car and begin the process of forgetting the day on the peaceful drive home.

Georgie and I spent a lovely evening on my pleasant screened porch. I splurged on some porch wicker and plush, deep white cushions with yellow striped pillows when I moved in. Curled at my side, she watches the butterflies and birds. I savor red wine and read a mindless piece of fiction where every character has to face numerous challenges with humor and grace. "A perfect end to the weekend," I tell myself as we move inside to PJs and my soft bed. She sleeps wherever she wants, and we are both content with that arrangement.

All too early, my phone alarm disrupts my sound sleep. Usually, my living alarm, Georgie, takes care of waking me up, but not today. The results being, I lie stunned, waiting for all my faculties to clear.

Georgie runs in and demands breakfast. Groggy, I feed and refresh her water and head straight to the shower to wake myself up. I pass by the closet, grab my work outfit, and watch mesmerized by the row of empty hangers swaying.

The sturdy wooden hanger held the blazer he wore on our first date. Navy blue, deep and bold, a color full of promise. A coat reminding me every time we entered the shared closet of where we started mingled with hints of where we would end.

Eyes tortured with unshed tears. Text pings in the oddest hours. Late work shifts more often than regular hours. Volunteering to travel more. The words not spoken say so much more than the ones we speak. We are fine, we tell ourselves, until we are not fine.

The hangers sway in the closet we once shared, the whole row empty of clothes I once washed and hung, moved out of my way, or carefully pressed. One hanger, wooden and strong, empty of the Navy blazer, swings in the open space as I slip to the floor and weep.

Everybody lies. Why did I take that journey down Memory Lane right now? I sigh out a breath, still the hanger, and move into the shower, letting the hot water wash over me. Can a tidal wave of sorrowful emotion be cleared away in the space of a 15-minute shower? I don't have time to process any of this. One thing I know for sure, thinking about the ultimate bittersweet time in my life won't help me one bit right now. Not one.

I rush through the rest of the morning routine and arrive at work on time. Now, I'm glad I worked some yesterday! I sweep my eyes over the parking lot, looking for the CW and/or Rascal, the orange tabby. If I were in my right mind, clear thinking and solid, I would find that feline and take it home with me—no sign of either one to distract my work plans or add to my distorted thinking.

Sometimes, I am my own best friend by not being in my right mind.

The day unfolds as a typical work day with my team on target and the work enjoyable. I move into a rhythm. We work like a flock of geese flying in formation. Laughter at the right spots in the day loosens any tension. I remind myself I do love my job just as much as I love to hate my job. When we all call it a day, I feel like a normal, sane woman again.

"Great job today, team! Enjoy your evening," I call out.

"You too!"

"See you tomorrow!"

My phone buzzes as I reach for it. Who is sending me a text?

'Hey, Vinca, this is Tony Garcia from Meadow's school. I think I can help with the problem you asked about. Uh...Hope you are doing well.'

This may be better than I imagined.

'Great!'

'Thumbs up'

'Smiley'

'Will call you when I have details, if that's okay?'

Call me? I guess.

'Sure.' I text back.

Well, that is one less thing for me to hyper-focus on. Tony will hopefully follow through. Just in case, I wrote on my calendar to text him on Friday. I make a new contact, and under his title, I put ticket helper. I leave on time. Determined to act on Meadow's Thanksgiving plan, I call Oakley for my driving home conversation.

"Hey, what's up?"

"Meadow sends her love and wants us to start a new Thanksgiving tradition. She already has plans to eat with Jonathan's family on

Thanksgiving Day, but she wants to come the weekend before with Caleb to have our own pre-holiday feast. How does that sound to you?"

"So, because she has made plans, we get to eat twice as much food? Not sure I follow that logic, but to have you three come out and spend the time with us will be worth it."

"Yeah, I didn't think about eating twice. What if we don't make our feast a turkey dinner, but an 'eat whatever the three of us want' meal? That might really be fun! We can even still have our traditional Thanksgiving breakfast before they need to leave. I don't have any other plans. Daddy and the two of us can eat all the leftovers for our dinner. We could bake a turkey breast if we wanted to be true Americans. Why don't you talk it over with him and see what he thinks?"

"I'm sure he will go along with anything that includes extra time with his grandson! Hey, thanks again for coming out. It meant a lot to Dad, and I needed to get the boat out. Kind of felt like we were teens again, right?"

"I loved it! I'm already kicking myself for taking so long to get back out to see you two. Daddy looking so frail and thin is a shock!"

We finished the ride home with the tale of the ticket for the biggest rule follower in history, me. I, once again, made the story funny and full of the emotion I felt as an entertaining escape from reality for my brother. I don't mention the anger I experienced. I don't mention the outrage from being falsely accused. I don't mention the frustration. The helplessness. The memories. I just make him laugh. Everybody lies.

Chapter 8
Rule Follower and Confrontation Hater

I decide to keep my ice cream date with Meadow and Caleb so that we can talk over the New Murray Thanksgiving Plans. Wednesday can't come soon enough!

Meadow lives in a sweet place perfect for her and Caleb. She and three of her Education Major friends decided that in their last year of college, they would teach close to each other and be roommates. They agreed to be a support team, with shoulders to lean on and independent of other support. They pored over places for rent and found the hundred-year-old house in need of TLC on the edge of the town center. The first time they saw how much TLC it needed, an idea began to form. They would ask for reduced rent in exchange for painting, repairs, and decorating the inside. They met with the homeowner, Eugene Landerford, a slow-moving gentleman who was recently widowed. He was so awed by their shared dream of teaching close, supporting each other, and educating the young that he readily agreed to their terms.

"Ladies, I think this is a win-win agreement for us all. I ask only that you submit to me in writing and/or drawing a plan of each job you plan to take on. I would also like a before-and-after picture. When we come to the end of our leasing agreement and you all move on, I may be able to get a penny or two for the place!"

"We all agree to your terms, and we also want to sit down with you in your kitchen over a meal we prepare and renegotiate the terms in one year," Meadow, ever the spokesperson, shares this caveat with Mr. Gene.

They have lived there for eight years, and the TLC they have provided has ranged from re-screening a porch to painting the exterior following the decrees of the Architectural Review Board. Mr. Gene was prophetic about the win-win, as their teacher salaries would not have made ends meet for any of them alone without a second income to help.

The large wrap-around porch, complete with porch swings on each end, says, "Sit awhile."

Over the years, the women have proposed and pitched additional renovations to Mr. Gene on his dime. Some he accepted, like the bathroom upgrades, some he put on the back burner for another time.

The porch with feather ferns in baskets, pots of deep fuchsia and white geraniums adds just the right balance. A set of French doors opens onto the porch from the dining room. A small table and chairs, set for breakfast, fit perfectly on the porch for the weekend mornings. I have spent a few Saturdays in the treasured spot myself.

Each woman has her own bedroom, with the Master bedroom reserved for guests. The small bedrooms have taken on the personality of the woman who sleeps there. When Meadow knew she was going to have Caleb, she took the room with a set of bunk beds. No matter how much the other women have tried to persuade her, she and Caleb are still in that room. He gets the top bunk and Meadow the bottom. The room is airy and fresh with white, shades of dark green, and accents of coral, his favorite color for now.

We meet there to walk together, taking advantage of the Indian summer day, hand in hand, Caleb in the center, swinging our arms and singing nonsense songs. We decide to each make something our Mamma used to make for our meal. We add a rule that we can make anything from any occasion or a regular, normal day.

"Oh, I forgot to tell you that Tony sent me a text about 'the problem' that he could help with," I share with her.

"Yeah, I wonder what he has in mind?" Meadow asks.

"He said he would call me."

"What? Oh, that is good. I mean, he's more of a text guy, not a call guy."

"Don't even start any of that! It's for one thing and one thing only-the ticket."

"Vinca, you need to branch out. Work. Oakley, Dad, Caleb, and I can't be your whole life forever!"

"I don't see why not! You four are safe, treat me well, and love me lots. What more do I need? Besides, time heals all wounds, and there has not been enough time to even start, much less finish. I have been having these weird memory sequences, like the red belt one. I had the half-empty closet one a few days ago when Chadwick left. I am fine. I walk into the half-empty closet and slide down the wall in tears. It was visceral. Still, after all this time, it was just as painful as it was all those years ago. What is happening to me?"

"You're human after all! I think you have probably repressed a lot of memories and moved into survival mode throughout your life. You were the protector, the one who took care of us all. You didn't dwell on what you were going through. You survived."

I think about all of this as we walk back to the house, ice cream slipping down the cones, our hands sticky with drips. Maybe she has a point about survival mode.

"Caleb, give Auntie V a big hug, the biggest one you have in you!" He wraps his arms and legs around me, and his ice-cream hands stick to my back as he pats me before I put him down.

" 'Night, Auntie V! See ya next week! Mommy, can I read one more chapter before I wash?"

"Sure, but at least wash your hands!" Meadow answers. "Love you, Big Sis! Keep in touch and drive safe!"

"Thank you for being you!"

"Let me know when Tony calls!"

"You are relentless!"

I drive home with a sweet smile on my face, the windows down, and the ideas for our new Thanksgiving flowing. I push the call button by my steering wheel and say, "Call Oakley mobile."

It goes right to voicemail. I know when he sees a call from me, he will call me back as soon as he can. I have so much love for Caleb, it makes me wonder if I will love my own child as much if I ever have the chance to be a mom. He's so full of wonder and the joy of living. His laugh from deep in that little boy belly just takes things to a deeper level of love. I feel peace around me as I drive. A deep sense of gratitude washes over me just as Oakley's alert comes in.

"Hey, Brother Oakley! I had the best ice cream date ever with our buddy nephew Caleb. Oh, he's such a little man! We talked over the Thanksgiving meal. What do you think about making foods that Mamma fed us? They don't even have to be Thanksgiving traditional."

"Oh, yeah. Wait, I have a whole menu idea in one pot with dessert included. You just inspired me! Low Country Boil and ice cream with choices of toppings and flavors!"

"Yes!"

"You and Meadow can bring the potatoes, corn, and kielbasa. Caleb and I'll throw the cast net and catch the shrimp. I've been wanting to teach him how to cast, so this is my chance. I'll get the ice cream and toppings. You'll have to tell me his favorites."

"I love it! We can probably come and spend Monday and Tuesday. Just in case you don't catch any shrimp, I can run to Edisto Fish market and get some."

"I really think we can handle it! But, if you want to have that as a backup plan, I'm all in. So, do you think Meadow will like that plan? Run it by her and get back to me. I loved it when we were growing up, and Pap and Mam would make the Lowcountry Boil for us. I know

Dad would enjoy that too. We can help teach Caleb how to make cocktail sauce and peel his own shrimp just like we learned.

"One day, you and I may even give him a cousin or two to share all this with! Not that I have anything in the works, just hoping, I guess."

"Funny, I was thinking about that earlier. Listen, I just pulled up, and I need to get inside and ready for bed. I'll let you know how Meadow feels, and we'll go from there. Love you!"

Chapter 9
Good Night and Good Riddance!

B etween and around all the work drama, I see a missed call from Tony. Now, a text would be inappropriate. I have to call him back. I hate to make phone calls. I mean, I really hate to make phone calls. Maybe I'll text him to let him know I saw he called. What good does that do me in finding out about him taking care of my problem? I hate this!

I resist the urge to text and don't really want to start that annoying phone tag. I hit call before I can talk myself out of it.

"Hello, Tony Garcia here."

"Hey, Tony, it's Vinca, Meadow's sister, the one with the problem she asked you to help me with?" I try laughing just a little to ease the tension.

"Hey! I guess you saw that I called earlier."

"Yeah, I was super focused at work today on a deadline of sorts and had my phone in my desk. I took a chance to call you back instead of texting. Honestly, I hate to call people!" I can't believe I just told him that! What the heck?

"I'm glad you called. I would not have answered if I weren't able to talk. I can laugh with you about hating things. I hate to introduce myself to people. Most of the time, they don't hear my name correctly, or they think I say Tom or Ted. Crazy." We both laugh a little more and start the rest of the conversation with the ease of friends.

"A brand-new cop on the force wrote the ticket. I talked to my supervisor. He took care of the fine and changed the offense, considering your stellar driving record. How in the world have you driven all this time without one ticket?"

"Well, besides hating to call people, I'm a definite rule follower, and the rules of the road matter to me." OMG, I sound like such a great person to be around, right?

"Listen, rules are what we all like, right? We might say we want to do whatever we want, but even kids like to know what is expected and what the consequences are if they break the rules. I see it every day in this school.

"Your sister seems to be a natural at finding the balance between too strict and too easy. Her students respect her! I hope this helps you with one less thing on your mind for the holidays."

"Yes, it does. I'm so grateful to you for speaking up for me. I was ready to go to court with diagrams and pictures of the road, testimony from my dad and others, maybe even the mayor, on my character and attention to the health and safety of others. Maybe even my Girl Scout Leader would have testified for me."

Tony laughs, a nice, hearty, sincere laugh, not just a polite laugh. I'm enjoying this conversation immensely. Imagine that.

"Well, it's been nice talking to you! I hope your Thanksgiving is nice."

"Yours too. Are you staying local or traveling?"

"We're going to be with our dad and brother about an hour away, so technically local. What about you?"

"I'm the official turkey fryer for my family. I do the frying at my house and have perfected the transport of a hot fried bird in a brown paper grocery bag wrapped inside a medium cooler. No fail, the birds stay hot and so tender, it melts in your mouth!"

"That sounds like quite the undertaking! We're opting for a pre-Thanksgiving feast with just the five of us and leftovers for

Thanksgiving Day. We always have Thanksgiving breakfast together, no matter what."

We pause a minute, thinking our thoughts of family and tradition, not quite ready to end the conversation.

"Thanks again, Tony, I owe you one! When I can think of an appropriate thank you, I will let you know." Did I really just say that?

"You're very welcome. You really don't owe me a thing, but I might take you up on whatever you come up with." WHAT?

We both laugh and say our goodbyes. I'm shocked at my flirting and a little proud I haven't forgotten how! I have a few more things to finish before I can leave for the day. One more reason why this job I love can also be this job I hate.

I love the team leadership role as we crank out ideas with each person toeing the line. I hate the times when someone slacks off or doesn't do a fair share of the work. I'm supposed to be the one who confronts, warns, redirects, and fires, if it comes to that. I hate confrontation almost as much as I hate making phone calls. My wandering mind grabs onto fourth-grade Vinca, and I relive her utterly devastating humiliation.

The time to use the restroom has come and gone. Rule three: Use the restroom and wash your hands quickly. Mrs. Taylor clearly states expectations with no exceptions. There was no need to do either when the class restroom time came up. There is a need now. My raised hand is ignored. My hand goes down as the pressure rises to a painful throbbing drum beat that cannot be ignored much longer. My hand flies up and shakes in the air, catching the eye of the Ignorer. Requesting to use the restroom when it is not time takes every ounce of strength I have. "No, it is not time. You should have gone a while ago." My hand falls. Shock and shame emerge into a hot mess of golden liquid splashing on the green tile, running down legs that tremble with rage and mix with the sobbing

tears as if a spotlight was shining. "WHY DIDN'T YOU SAY IT WAS AN EMERGENCY? GO TO THE OFFICE AND CALL HOME." Rushed into the hallway, crushed, hearing the voice of a friend telling all the mean-teasing kids, "She threw up. She can't help that." Everybody lies.

I snap back into reality as if I never left. The memory took me back to when I was nine and could not confront old Mrs. Taylor, to my horror and shame. As the angst sinks in deeply, my hands shake and my legs weaken. The tears start, shocking and visceral. I cry for little girl Vinca. What is happening to me? Why do I keep remembering, not just a random thought, but a real in-body replay?

I sit in my rocker mindlessly drifting for so long that it has gotten completely dark. The recent fall-back time change results in darkness coming on so suddenly.

"This is ridiculous! Enough already. Enough!" I tell myself.

I texted Meadow, 'Call me when you can.'

She replies, 'thirty minutes'

I head to the shower, allowing the hot water to wash over me. I come back to myself in a weary, refreshing way. I dig out my favorite PJs, put on my favorite show to binge, and wait for her call.

She calls right on time. I let her in on Oakley's idea, and she loves it, every part of it. We make plans, adding in details and taking them away, before I tell her about Tony.

She teases me, and we laugh over our awkward back and forth and flirting in between. I tell her I do feel like I owe him something in thanks. She promises she will help me come up with just the right something. I hear a loud call from Caleb wanting another chapter of <u>Wonder</u> before he goes to bed. I don't tell her about going back in time-trance to 4th grade. I don't say a word.

Chapter 10
Ready to Pounce

The week before a holiday feels like a dragon and an ox fighting for speed, and no one wins. I decided to work hard and get ahead so that I can take the whole Thanksgiving week off. I may stay at the family house all week long. I'm waiting until I get there and experience the tension, or lack of tension, first. The very thought of the house evokes so many memories, and I may need those extra days to myself. Can I take Daddy drinking and smoking like Oakley does? Can I be in that house and not miss Momma, Pap, and Mam like an ache that never stops? I know I haven't gone through the boxes of old photos in the trunk that sits like a sentinel guarding the hallway to the porch. We used to sit for hours and look at the photos, laughing at the people we were kin to but never knew. I can at least make a start and split the pictures into three stacks for our generation to keep.

Meadow was the one who took almost all of the recent photos. She picked up one of Mom's cameras, and that was all it took for someone to see she had the eye for photography. There's a shot of baby Caleb sitting stock still, looking at our cat, looking at him. Both are transfixed by the other and are trying to cast a spell that will last. The shot does poetic justice to a cat and a little boy. What is not shown is the next frame, when the cat leaped on Caleb's head with its baby claws out, grabbing for hair, until he launched the cat airborne into the ceiling fan. He landed with a thud, stunned for a moment, recovered, and darted away. She took lovely shots of Momma and Daddy, some of the last ones of them together.

As I walk out to my car to leave for the day, I catch a glimpse of the orange tabby. The urge to capture that kitten calls to me to take action. I have to put some kibble in a nice dish next to my car, grab it, and drive off. I'll bet it needs shots and flea treatment, probably a good vet visit, and of course, spaying or neutering is a must-do. It will probably love my condo, and Georgie will have a playmate during the long days when I work.

While I think up all these plans, I follow the small speed demon all the way to the edge of the park, where, you guessed it, CW stands like a statue in her favorite and only outfit. I don't know if it is the holiday, the time-trances, or her repeated phrase, but before I can talk myself out of it, I speed up even faster straight toward her.

"Hello!"

Nothing. Just staring.

"Um, Ma'am, are you okay?" I shout and keep my distance as the wind picks up. I catch a whiff of her fragrance, unwashed and stale.

No reply at all. I don't know what to do in this impulsive chase after the cat. I didn't expect a close encounter with the CW.

"Do you need help?" I shout. Why? What can I possibly do to help her? What will I say if she says 'yes'? Geez, what is up with me?

She tilts her head slightly to the right. Her hands move up to her face as if she has just awakened from sleep. I'm at a complete stop, still as a stone, staring at her. The scene unfolds as she opens her pocket, and once again, the tabby comes running to climb inside.

The kitten must burrow down because if I had not just witnessed the scene, I would have no idea the CW is carrying a cat. She hyper-focuses on me just like she was staring into space a few minutes ago.

A chill wind runs up and down my spine. My feet, as if cemented to the sidewalk, render me immobile. Every fight or flight nerve in my body jumps to attention. Ready to run and unable to move, battle for victory. Crystal clear and focused, I notice details in snippets like a series of Meadow's photos.

Her eyes, crystal ice blue, piercingly focused, lock on my hazel ones with an intensity that doesn't seem possible for her size. Her slender nose, red and running, makes me think she must have a cold or worse. Her mouth, set in a determined grimace, all at once lifts at the corners into a smile. Her face, transformed by the smile, becomes tranquil, and her eyes glow. I still can't move. I still stare as if I'm waiting for her to answer. Am I?

"Everybody lies," she says softly around her smiling mouth, "Everybody!"

She turns on her heels and walks away from me faster than I have ever seen an older woman move. I still can't make my feet work. I can't make my voice call after her either. All I can do is look around to see if anyone else witnessed this strange encounter and shake my head.

I take two deep inhales and exhales, counting slowly, and my feet are back with me. I sprint back to the parking lot of my office like I do every day with an 'I am fine' attitude and 'I did not have an encounter with a CW and a cat that was over the top weird'. By the time I fling open my car door, slam it shut, and punch the lock button, I feel close to hyperventilating. No longer able to take the deep breaths, I pant my way into starting up the car and moving in any direction as fast as I can safely drive. I call my sister, of course, I do.

"Hey Via! Nice to hear from you again. It's been so long since we talked," she teases.

"Meadow, I'm losing it. Seriously, losing it."

"Well, that's not news to me. I could have told you that a long time ago!"

"Listen to me!" To my horror, my voice catches, and I hear her take in a breath.

"Sorry, really. Go ahead. What happened?"

"You know that feral orange kitten I told you about and we laughed and laughed over the Crazy Woman?"

"Yeah, I mean, I remember, and it was funny."

"Meadow, she really is crazy!" I proceed to recount the story, and Meadow listens as a good sister does, putting in all the right comments throughout. She doesn't give me advice but asks me questions. I'm certain there are skills she learned in some "Be A Positive Listener" teacher training class she took.

"Why did you chase after the cat? What were you planning to do? What made you call out to the woman?"

Notice that she doesn't call her the CW, to preserve her dignity and not to judge or stereotype.

I reply in my worst annoyed tone of voice.

"If I knew the answers to those questions, I would not have acted impulsively and run after the cat, nor would I have had the whole weird encounter in the first place! Thank you very much for all your wonderful help."

Click.

I drive the rest of the way home seething with annoyance, indignation, and frustration. I never saw Meadow's text she sent right after school until I walked in my door and set my phone on the counter.

'BTW, ran into Tony today, rather he made a point of running into me. He says you had a nice conversation, and you said you owe him. Just what do you have in mind, Sis?'

She manages to make me smile a little before I end this awful day. I light some candles and set them along the edge of the tub as it fills with the lavender stress relief soak Caleb gave me for my birthday. As I walk back and forth getting my soft PJs, pulling my hair up, setting all my after-bath things in order, pouring a tall glass of water, I determine not to deal with the day anymore. I am done.

I sink into the tub, close my eyes, and embrace the mesmerizing effect of the flickering candles through my lids. I raise my glass, "Here's to you, CW, and your feral tabby! You can't get to me anymore tonight. Good night, and good riddance!"

Chapter 11
The Eyes Behind the Smile

I start stacking piles of clothes to take to Adams Run a little at a time, so I don't forget anything. I always put a notepad on the corner of the counter to add to my list as I walk by the kitchen about a week before any trip I take. I tell myself how efficiently I pack, and for this trip, casual is all I need. I like to put in one thing slightly above casual, just in case an unforeseen opportunity arises. I have my own made-up method I created after watching "How To Pack for a Ten-Day Trip in One CarryOn" videos.

I pick three colors only so that I can mix and match with minimal effort or items. Just seeing the pile grow makes the work days fly by. All I have left to do is purchase my corn and potatoes, as Meadow will supply the kielbasa and make the cocktail sauce for our Lowcountry Boil.

I'm taking Georgie with me for the whole week. She'll have the ability to roam around the house and come and go as she pleases. It's like a cat vacation spa resort for her. Plenty of safe places to explore and not enough danger to really hurt her. Besides, she loves Daddy's lap. Caleb loves her, but shows love by trying to catch her, carry her, and make her fetch, all of which she loathes as only a cat can. The cat's evil eye will be flashed more than once, I'm sure.

Thoughts of the tabby and the CW still linger around the edges of my mind. I shove them back. Not now. Not today. That bizarre woman and her feral beast are surely fine and well in their park existence in our great small town of Summerville. I mean, who would hurt an old lady and a kitten, right?

Tony has also managed to enter and exit my thoughts as well. He told Meadow I said I owe him one, so that must mean he found the idea of payback intriguing in a weird sort of way. He was flirting with me as much as I was flirting with him. Actually, phone flirting is much nicer than in-person flirting in so many ways. Use your voice, use your mind, but no body language, no fear of crossing the line because any line crossed can be safely uncrossed with a sign off. We were definitely phone flirting.

I now have all the stacks ready and will soon move them to the carry-on case. Last things last, I pick out a nice, silky blouse and some black jeans with my most comfortable booties for my just-in-case outfit. I can still pack with the best of the best. As I put each stack in the case, I grab up my undies and bras and think back to that first miserable bra that I had to wear. Momma was the one who told me what was up with the Facts of Life talk.

"Vinca, it is time," she began.

"Time for what?"

"Time for you to sit down and shut your mouth, young lady!"

"Why did you call me that?"

"Because you are. Now, don't ask me another question until I'm finished. This is hard enough to say without you asking a million things before I can explain it all, so sit."

I sat. I shut my mouth. It really was that simple.

"You're growing up into a woman. Right now, you're a young woman whose body is changing. You're going to take a shower when we finish this talk, and I'm going to take you to buy your first bra."

My eyes were saucers. I couldn't believe what she was saying. Her face was a deep shade of red, and she held my hand, gently rubbing my thumb with hers. My first bra? My first bra? MY FIRST BRA! My mind spoke as my mouth was directed to shut up.

"I'm sorry I didn't notice this before. In your white shirt in the sunlight, I can clearly see the buds growing."

My mouth dropped open, but I kept any words from leaving. Somehow I have buds growing?

"They need to be covered for modesty and to keep you from being so sore when they grow larger and fuller. You will get two training bras. I'll help you adjust them," she glances at my face and notices for the first time how mortified I am at her words.

"Oh, Vinca, don't be the drama queen right now! There's more that I have yet to say. Suck it up and take it in. Just know every single girl turns into a young woman before she becomes a woman. You will be strong. You will be proud one day. Right now, it will just feel as awkward as this conversation we're trying to have. Say, 'Okay, Momma,' so I know you hear me."

"K, Mom," I squeak out.

She gives me the Tiger Eye, and I swallow for another try, "Okay, Momma." I give her a pasted-on smile and grit my teeth.

"Very soon, you will also change in other ways. I was twelve when this happened to me. God made a woman to have children. This is a very important job. Our female bodies start getting us ready for this when we turn into young women."

I stare at her incredulously. Never in a million years can I even imagine anything more horrible than turning into a young woman. I am not ready for this. My belly churns. That horrible sensation deep in my bowels that yells, "Get me to a toilet!" rises. In fact, the double whammy of throwing up or having diarrhea began a battle surrounded by my mother's detailed description. Her beautiful face is so serious and intense, her deep brown eyes filled with tears unshed, telling of the emotion she experiences trying to explain the facts of life to her girl, who is on the edge of Young Womanhood. I nod a few times my tongue stuck to the roof of my mouth telling myself not to throw up or have the runs.

"You will make a lining in your body for a baby to grow. If no baby is inside you, you will release this lining out of your body."

"Momma, stop! This is too much, I don't want a baby to grow in me! You can have another baby, not me. I saw how you grew with Meadow, no, no ma'am ...I (sob) just (sob)can't."

She looks at me with her best mother look that says more than any word ever could, when she points her index finger at me and hisses my entire name.

"Vinca Joyland Murray..."

I'm done for.

"Having sex with a young man is the only way for a baby to grow inside you. You will not be having sex with any young man until you are much older and wiser. I will help you when that time comes."

I have recovered enough just to sniffle now, and the hiccups start. I shake my head no, but know better than to make a verbal sound of protest. She takes a deep breath, sits up straight and tall, preparing to torture me some more.

"Your body gets ready every month just in case you are going to have a baby. Every month, the lining will release. Many people call this your period. It is a period of time when the lining releases."

That explains what I heard our sitter talking about one time! Can this get any worse?

"It looks like brownish blood and releases into your undies."

Yes, yes, it can. Oh, yes, it really can. I leak out a few noiseless tears. She relentlessly continues.

"You will need to tell me when this happens, so I can help you with what you need. I'll get supplies for you and show you how to use them. They are pads that stick to your undies, and the lining will be absorbed into them. You will change these every few hours. You may not start your period for a year, or it could be sooner. Because you have started budding, that is the first sign you are becoming a young woman. Vinca, I know this is a lot, but you will get through it."

She wraps me in a tight hug, sniffs once, and sends me to the shower. I stand topless in front of the mirror, take a long look at my buds. Something is starting to grow! One is budding before the other, but it is happening! Oh, I'm so not ready for all this. Will I have one big boob and one small? Why?

All this anguish preceded the ultimate embarrassment as we went to purchase the new bra. The packages labeled Training Bra looked like neon lights to me, sitting at the bottom of the Target shopping cart. Between putting things on top of them until we got to the checkout and reliving the conversation about sex with a young man and a baby growing in the lining, I was one overwhelmed girl.

I sigh with the memory deep and abiding, even more poignant as I zip the carry-on and roll it to the door. I'm almost ready for the plethora of memories this trip home with the Mixed, the White, and the Black Murray Sibs will surely evoke.

After a quick run for groceries, I take one walk through the condo. Georgie settles in her crate as the last item I add to the fully packed car, ready for the time away together. I expect nothing. I find that if I can lower my bar, I'll be better off and protected rather than hoping for everything to be great. I have choices to stay one night or many. I don't have to decide until I have to decide. I start the car up, turn the tunes up, and text Oakley that I'm on my way.

The soft light of the mid-morning soothes me as I sing the old songs that can mix and mingle with the memories just right and not too acrid anymore. I slip in and out of the cars with my window halfway down, relishing the crisp fall blue sky so pure and perfect. But really, that training bra! Was there anything more torturous? When I wore it to school and the boys dared each other to pop the back band, I was furious! I mean, how dare they?

I drive with the ease of the familiar. The tension releases as the trees send me into a place of peace, almost complete.

"Georgie cat, we are soon going to be at your best cat Spa ever."

She answers me with a stilted meow sound like a squeaky door slowly opening. I can hear her purr mingling in.

"Yes, you old sweet thing, we are going home. Not sure what that will mean or how long we will stay. But it will be at least one night and one meal. If you behave, we might treat you to a shrimp or two. Not much longer now."

I let my mind drift, and the CW and her tabby flash into my thoughts like unwanted visitors who will not take the hint to leave. I shake them away with a toss of my hair, lowering my window all the way. Inhaling the pungent pluff mud reaches into the soul of a person like an intimate, profound healing. I am going home. Still, the flashes of tabby and the ice blue eyes linger around the edges of my mind, not quite sharp and clear, but niggling and ready to pounce.

Chapter 12

Borrowing Trouble

Oakley meets me at the car and starts unloading my suitcase, overnight bag, Georgie's crate, food bowls, kibble and groceries.

"Nice to see you are going to stay awhile, but I don't know if Daddy and I can stand you for a year!"

"I know, but I finally settled on I'll stay for our family dinner and spend at least one night, but I might decide to stay for a few extra days since I'm off all week."

"That makes sense in a Vinca kind of way."

"Look, don't tell Daddy yet. I need to see how things pan out before I commit. Okay?"

He lifts the last bag of groceries, and I grab Georgie's crate, talking sweetly to her as he and I walk inside. We make our way to the kitchen.

"Okay," he gives me a sideways hug. My brother has always been my stability. I feel a huge stab of love hit my core.

"I appreciate all you have done for me. Just know that!"

"Ahh, you are my big Sis. What choice did I have?"

We both laugh as we put the grocery items away and chatter about nothing important.

"I was thinking..." I begin easing into the hard conversation.

"Oh no, I'm in trouble now." I bop him lightly on the shoulder.

"No, really? I think it's time for us to look through the old photo chest together. I mean, Daddy knows who a lot of the people are that we have no idea about. We can start with a stack and have him identify people. I can record on the back what he says."

"That sounds like a good idea, but keeping it small is important. We need to make sure we don't overwhelm Daddy. Maybe after Caleb goes to bed?" he replies.

"I want to see if there are any in there of Grand Pap, Mamma, Momma, and her siblings when they were small. I think Caleb might like to see them, too. I mean, one day, all of this will probably be his. At the rate you and I are going, he may be the only grandchild of this generation of ours."

"I have you know, I have not given up, and you shouldn't either!"

"Well, at least one of us has some hope. I don't know, Oakley. I've become rather cynical when it comes to men and trusting people. I'm so over people lying to me! I take it personally every time, like all the world looks at me and says, 'Here's a sucker we can take advantage of so easily' with one little lie. One leads to another, and before I know it, I believe them all. Then, they drop me like a disgusting, filthy cleaning rag. Everybody lies!"

I can't believe I just quoted the CW to my brother! The unease I felt earlier in the car rushes into my veins, and I divert my attention to Georgie.

"Time to let this one enjoy her Cat Spa! Forget all that I just vented to you."

I open the French doors to the screen porch first, giving her time to explore freely and reacquaint herself with the house she has visited since I first got her. She sniffs every plant, corner, and cranny, and settles in a beam of direct sunlight. She stretches out with eyes closed in the ultimate cat pose of utter contentment pre-nap. I envy her!

Daddy comes into the room, pushing his walker with a grin and a greeting.

"I thought I heard a commotion in my otherwise peaceful domicile! Look at that sweet Georgie enjoying the best life a cat could have! Come over here and give your old man some love."

I wrap my arms gently around him, planting a kiss on his bristly cheek, inhaling his familiar scent of sweat, cigarette, and strong soap combined into a paradox of love. I look at him covertly, distracting him with small talk and cat antics to laugh over.

When I was growing up, he was the strongest man alive. His arms could lift me from the car into my bed, even when I was too old to be carried, and I would pretend to be asleep so he would carry me in anyway. He could calm the worst nightmare I had. He always checked my terror of sounds I thought I heard and creepy things that might be hiding, waiting to attack. I would catch the scent of him first and see him second. Now, his frail arms work so hard to move himself forward on unsteady feet. His face, thin and stretched, shows etching of wisdom around his eyes and the corners of his mouth. When he grins at me or the cat, these smooth away, and he is Daddy again, just slimmer and older.

"Did you bring Meadow and Caleb? Where are they hiding?"

"No, Daddy, they're driving separately, so they can leave in time to have Thanksgiving dinner with Jonathan's family."

"I admit, I was hoping they might change their plans and stay here longer. I understand that Caleb needs to know his father's people, too, even if Jonathan's not actually there. Don't let me get started on that sore subject! Anyway, I'm glad to see you, my number one daughter, Vinca, my Flower Bud!"

We spend the afternoon in the easy rhythm of families, with each of us napping, reading, and relaxing. We take time to walk out on the lawn and dock, and just be to ourselves together as naturally as breathing. We are biding our time waiting for Caleb and Meadow to arrive so we can garnish the love energy that only a six-year-old can provide. I love seeing Daddy and Caleb together. Each of their faces reflects the light off the other in that bond between men as grandfather to grandson.

The three of us sit on the porch in the afternoon sun, with the cat's antics chasing leaves to distract us. The smoke rings Daddy blows in three circles as he did when I was young fascinate me and sicken me as this habit of his takes another bit of his life away.

"You are showing off for Caleb, Daddy!" I tease him.

"Guilty as charged!" he agrees as he sips his cold drink. I'm counting how many he has consumed, determined that Caleb will get the best of sober Grand Pap I can produce.

We hear the driveway sing as Meadow's old VW runs over the loose oyster shells. Before she can put the car in park and turn off the engine, Caleb's door flies open, and he runs full on to jump into my arms. He has been doing this as a test to see how long Auntie V can catch him without toppling over. He wraps his body around mine. I plant both feet firmly on the ground. Our laughter runs around us, and he slips out of my arms in awe that I can still catch him.

Daddy watches from the porch as Oakley twirls Meadow around in a complete 360. His pale skin held against her mellow darkness beautifully blends as our family is together in all our tones and mixes: the Murray three, the old man original, and the single offshoot together in our family home.

Caleb sees Daddy and drops to his feet, ready to run full on at him. His face registers the walker, and he pulls back to take it all in.

"Hello, my favorite grandchild of all the grandchildren ever born! Don't I get one of those Caleb hugs?"

"Auntie V, can I still hug him?" he whispers in my ear.

"Sure you can! Go to the side of him and put your arms around his middle. Be easy and soft."

He runs up the steps and skids to a stop just in time to follow my instructions. The three of us watch in love and awe at the oldest and youngest together. Meadow quietly snaps a photo. I look forward to seeing what else she finds to capture on this first early Thanksgiving Murray Tradition.

Daddy ruffles Caleb's hair. His voice rises and falls in laughter, excitement, and absolute awe as Daddy blows the smoke rings.

"Listen, kid. Don't start this habit, okay. Promise your old Grand Pap that you will never smoke anything."

"Grand Pap, I promise...what you said."

"No. No. You've got to stand up like a young man and say the words. Try again."

"Okay, Grand Pap. I will not smoke."

"Anything."

"Anything."

"Never."

"Never."

We unpack the car and put away the groceries, leaving them to their own devices.

"You both tried to tell me that Daddy was getting worse, but I wasn't prepared to see him so thin and attached to that walker. Oakley, how can you let him smoke? And drink?"

"Meadow, please, don't start. Come on, you just got here. I promise time to talk about all of this, but for now, can we be a family? For Caleb's sake?"

The anger leaves her face, and she sighs out weakly, "Okay, but this enabling is so ridiculous."

Oakley and I lock eyes over her head and form a silent pact to stay quiet. We have had time with Daddy to acclimate; she has not.

"Caleb, are you ready to help me catch some shrimp?"

"Yes, I was born ready!" We all laugh and look at Meadow.

"No idea where that came from!"

Oakley takes Caleb for a piggyback ride to the edge of the dock, complaining loudly.

"You've grown so much and gotten so heavy, I can hardly carry you anymore."

"Auntie Via can still pick me up! You might need to try some of her Pilates," he suggests. We laugh, pull up chairs on the lawn, to watch the magic unfold.

A cast net, the first real fishing implement for many Lowcountry natives, presents a graceful dance as it opens in a full circle before it hits the water. If the caster does not know the finesse of throwing the net, it will flop and close before any chance of catching a shrimp happens. Oakley has a small version ready to instruct Caleb. As soon as I see it, I know it is the very same one we all learned how to throw on this dock over the years. Oakley and I were taught by our Grand Pap, so was Daddy, the Baltimore White son-in-law, who married his beautiful daughter. Daddy taught Meadow as Grand Pap had passed on by her sixth birthday.

"The first step is to shake out the net so all the sinkers are at the bottom end and the rope point is at the top." The thumping staccato of the weights on the wood sings a familiar tune.

"Next, you hold that point in your left hand and fan out one side, like this." Oakley stoops down to pick up the next edge between two sinkers. Caleb watches and listens as if he must conquer this on the first try. I suppose all those years of telling him one day you will throw the cast net just like us have kicked in.

"Okay, now this is the tricky part that proves if you are a real man or a real woman. You put this edge in your mouth, like this." He takes the string part and slips it in between his teeth. Unable to talk clearly, he mumbles out directions.

"You pick up the edge and make a circle. Throw across your body, opening your mouth just so, as the net opens in that beautiful circle," He follows these instructions by demo, releasing a cast with the form and grace of an expert. The net submerges perfectly.

"See? Next, you pull on the rope here to close the net around Mr. Shrimpy and all his Shrimpy relatives and friends. Shrimp are bottom feeders, so they hang out on the bottom of the creek. I'll pull this up to see if we have anything this time."

He pulls on the rope, and as it closes, he draws it toward him. The forms of life caught in the mesh of the net wriggle and reflect the sunlight. We stand up and clap, uncertain if we have shrimp or not, but we can see we have something. Oakley drops the net open on the dock. He and Caleb sort through the wriggling, flapping mess, releasing any small fish or crabs that they captured and putting the few shrimp in a bucket.

"Mamma, look! Here's a shrimp!" Before we can stop him, he tries to pick one up, and the barb catches him on the back of his hand.

"Ahhhh, it bit me. That shrimp actually bit me!" He jumps up and down, and we all good-naturedly laugh.

"Come on, you know better than to try to pick up a live shrimp! Let me see. Okay, my nephew, you are now an official shrimper, and your net awaits."

"Awww. Not sure how I'll do now with an injury and all. Maybe you should cast and let me sort."

"No way! I'll help you every step of the way. You are six now, and six is the perfect age for this net. Ready?"

"I guess."

"Try again. Ready?" We all laugh at the determined look on Caleb's face.

"Ready!" He takes the net and smiles from ear to ear.

They spend a few hours taking turns. We won't need to make a trip to Edisto Seafood Market to buy shrimp for this dinner. He even helps Oakley head the shrimp before he is ready to quit. I think it must be in the DNA. We have a true Lowcountry Boy.

"I miss Momma. The intensity surprises me. She would have loved this tradition. I feel her presence everywhere as if she is here with us in spirit," I say to Meadow.

"Yes, coming home is really coming back to those memories, right?" she responds.

"I thought we could start looking through the photos. You know, let Daddy identify the people we have no idea about and write their names on the back. Even if we get to a few, that will be a start."

"As one who loves to take pictures, it's awful to think someone may find them one day and have no idea who the people are. That's fine with me, if we wait until Caleb falls asleep."

We all head to the house to wash up and start the supper.

The best thing about Lowcountry Boil is one pot for cooking, one pot to clean. All you need is a large pot, some Old Bay Seasoning, a big colander, and some brown paper grocery bags, and you are set for your easiest meal ever. Oakley has unearthed the special cooker our Grand Pap welded when he worked for the Charleston Naval Shipyard. It was his pride and joy. It's a burner attached to a propane tank and fits perfectly on the pot base. The water is set to boil, and the Old Bay is added. How much to add is up to the cook. We eyeball it rather than measure.

When it looks right and the water is boiling, in go the small red potatoes. Adjust the amounts of all the ingredients for your crowd of eaters. Set a timer for ten minutes, then add your ears of corn on the cob. Over the years, we have shortened this step to frozen corn so we don't have to shuck, chop, and clean corn ourselves. Our grandparents would be ashamed of us! Set the ten-minute timer again. When that chimes, add the sliced chunks of kielbasa for the family members who might not eat shrimp. Set that timer for ten more minutes, and in goes the best ingredients of all, the stars of the creek, shrimp. We add ours with the peelings on because part of the fun of eating Lowcountry Boil is peel-and-eat shrimp. Now, you have to keep an eye on this step, because they cook fast and turn to rubber just as fast. As soon as they turn from grey to a lovely pink, they are ready.

Pour all of this mixture into the strainer. Shake it up a few times. Take shifts if you are making it for a crowd. Have those brown grocery bags spread out on a flat surface, then pour that delicious concoction from the strainer out on the bags. The steam will rise to entice you to nibble, but all that brew is extremely hot, so grab the cocktail sauce and call the others first. Be sure to include an extra plate for the shrimp peelings, butter for the corn and potatoes, and plenty of hand wipes. All of this goes down well with sweet tea or cold beer.

Caleb is so proud of the catch of shrimp that he can hardly eat them. He keeps looking for the biggest one and claiming that as one he got in the net, not Unk O, his name for Oakley.

"Caleb, you did a great job today. You showed us you can listen and learn. You showed us you kept trying even when you weren't successful at first. I'm proud of you, Grand Boy, very proud." Daddy smiles at him, and Caleb beams.

"Grand Pap, how long did it take you to learn how to catch shrimp?"

"Your Great Grand Pap taught me how. Let me tell you, he was a good teacher. See, he was not quite sure he liked me at first. When your Great Momma brought me here to meet him, he kept calling me the White Baltimore Boy even though I was a doctor, and I loved his daughter with all my heart! I had to show him I was okay for a White Baltimore Boy, and that just took time. A long time.

"Anyway, the first test was to learn how to catch shrimp. He was tricky, too! He took me out on a very sunny day, maybe on purpose, maybe not, but I had no sunscreen on this white skin of mine, and he didn't need it like I did. I wouldn't admit I was frying my hide, and he wouldn't either. I think I turned into a red lobster that day! Your Grand Momma was furious with him!"

We all laughed at the same story we had heard on repeat from him whenever we ate shrimp. I reached over to peel a shrimp for Caleb. Daddy lightly slapped my hand.

"No, no, no, Viabud! Once a man catches shrimp in a cast net, he has to peel his own shrimp! It's only right. Put that one down, and let him try. Okay, Caleb, hold it by the tail. Run your thumb between all of its little swimmers, like this. Then, see that clear crackly shell? Break it away and pull that sweet fella out. Dip him in the cocktail sauce and eat the food of the gods!" He slurps a shrimp noisily into his mouth. There is nothing sweeter than a fresh catch.

"Wait a minute! What about dessert? Mom said we would have ice cream with lots of toppings!"

We groan, laced with laughter, and set up a Sundae bar with lots of colorful choices on the best vanilla ice cream churned fresh every day. Not to be outdone, I add the hot fudge with whipped cream and a cherry on top.

We eat until our bellies are full. The laughter, kidding, old stories, and new tales mix with the salt-scented air. They stir around us, enveloping us in love, so much love. We watch the sun set as the sky releases all the colors of deep fall into purple, then navy blue, into the night. The stars start to pop, and Caleb fights being tired.

"Come on, Buddy, let's say good night to everyone and get you settled in." Meadow sees how tired he really is.

"Ah, Mamma! I'm not tired at all..." he whines as she gently but firmly takes his hand.

"Let's go, my tired, young man! I'll be back in a bit to help clean up."

We move to the comfortable chairs of the porch, and Dad lights up. So much of me wants to scream at him 'What are you doing?', but I don't. Not wanting to stir up any trouble, I sigh and start to bag up the leftovers. Oakley folds up the paper bags for the trash and cleans the table top. He fills the pot with soapy water for later. We join Dad on the porch in the dark. I flip on a lamp and bring a handful of the photos from the trunk into the room.

"Daddy, would you be up for looking through these old pictures to tell us who the people are in these photos? Do you feel like you can do this?"

"Maybe I mean, I know I can, but I am not sure if I want to. How many are we talking about here? That trunk is full!"

"I know it is. I have a small stack, ones that I thought you would know about in some way. If they start to be too much, we'll stop. I just think it's so important for us to do this for Caleb so he knows who his people are."

"Oakley, bring me another liquid courage, son. If I'm going to do this picture ID stint, I need all the courage I can muster."

I roll my eyes so only Oakley can see. Meadow joins us laughing and sharing how many times Caleb asked for one more page of Wonder before he fell asleep. She glows. As happy as I am for her, I'm jealous and petty, too. Will I ever feel that shimmering level of contentment?

"What did I miss?" Meadow inserts as we start flipping through the photos, passing one to another and finally to Daddy, who nonchalantly passes back to me with a positive ID and a little bit of background elaboration. We find many of our Great Aunts and some of our cousins once removed. My dad's sharp memory, a negative on so many levels, is a bonus now. How many times must he have looked at these photos with his wife's family, the beautiful black woman he called Angel? I jot down notes on the back and add his tidbits too. He pauses and fixes his entire attention on one photo, staring longer than any of the others. We all three stop our assembly line, glance at each other, and shrug. We wait. We wait longer.

"This is your Momma, my Angel, and her siblings, your future Auntie Grace and Uncles Tobias, Luther, and Marcus. The traditional obligatory family photo in front of the Azalea bushes on Easter morning." He passes the photo but does not pick up another one. The puzzled look mirrored on all our faces asks, "Why did this photo stop you?"

"Look at that one closely. See your mother holding that Easter stuffed rabbit as if her life depended on it. Look how Grace has her arm around her. Are any of them smiling? Do any of the others have a toy or treat? What you don't see is that your Pap drank all the Easter treat money, and your mom was the only one who got a treat that year. What you don't see is that he never came home that night. In fact, they had no idea if he was even alive on that Blessed Easter Morn. If you dig around in the chest of bitter memories, you'll find a picture of you three standing just like this with those same grimaces that pose for a smile, Meadow holding on to her basket. No sign of me, because I was nowhere to be found on that Blessed Easter morn either. Your precious Angel of a Momma grew up with the devil of alcoholism and married him, too.

"I'm done. Goodnight, my children, that's who Caleb's people are. That's who your people are. Look closely at what you are asking, Vinca. Look closely at the eyes behind the smiles."

He drains his beverage, lights up one last smoke, and glides his walker inside.

Chapter 13
Denial Wins Again

We linger a while and absorb what Daddy shared. Every family has its dysfunction, I suppose. I have no memory of Grand Pap drinking like that. I don't remember Momma sharing with me. I wonder what else I don't know about my mother, Annalise Rosemay Pringle. Everybody lies, indeed.

I tell them both more details of the CW and the orange kitten. I do my best storytelling ever. We're all laughing at the bizarre happenings. Somehow, I omit the everybody lies line the CW says to me every time I see her. That illustrates me as the protector, entertainer, rescuer of my siblings, the oldest kid. I have perfected it quite well. Denial wins again.

We talk over our plans for Thanksgiving breakfast and when Meadow and Caleb will be heading out to make it to Jonathan's family gathering on time. Meadow planned ahead by putting together a breakfast casserole. All we have to do is pop it in the oven.

"Listen, you two, I have a challenge for you!" Meadow starts resplendent in her teacher mode.

"What are you even doing?" I reply.

"Haven't we had enough challenges for today? You have no idea how difficult it is to make it look like Caleb caught more shrimp than me," Oakley adds.

"Yes, this is a request from me and Caleb, so if you let me down, you devastate him." We both moan in anticipation of what she is going to ask us to do.

"We want each of you to invite someone to join you for Thanksgiving Dinner."

"Oh, no, how Hallmark-movie can you get?"

"There are a number of people right here in Adams Run who are alone. Just ask them. Each of you, Daddy, too, ask one person. You have more than enough Lowcountry Boil for three more people. There's even ice cream and toppings left for dessert." She puts up her hand in the universal sign language of say no more.

"I have spoken, and it shall be. And I speak for Caleb, too. Now, you two have a head start, as it's not too late to ask someone tonight. Or you can wait until the morning and give Daddy the same parameters as you both have. Don't let me down! Or Caleb. He wants to interview you all over the weekend to hear your version of the story. He has an idea of a great way to share this."

Oakley opens his mouth. Meadow holds up both hands. We all laugh and hug in a huddle, each moving to our childhood rooms to settle in for the night. I decided to wear my good outfit for tomorrow's meal and our mystery guests. I hang up my blouse before I slip into bed for a deep, contented sleep.

The savory aroma of Meadow's casserole mingles with coffee and reaches my asleep self as the best wake-up call ever. My stomach growls as I snuggle Georgie up to my face and linger over her purrs. The wake-up sounds enter my room through the half-open window. The air, edged with just the right chill, makes for the best sleep ever. The birds begin their varied chirps and chatters. The wind blows over the tea olives, sending in the fresh scent of nature at its best.

"Well, my queen Cat, who will I invite for Thanksgiving dinner? Who would want to come for Lowcountry Boil instead of tradition?"

Georgie just purrs and mews and rubs her head on my hand before rolling on her back for a belly rub. Oh, the life of a cat! I think about Daddy's neighbors and sort out that's where we should start our quest for guests. I throw back the covers and make my way downstairs.

I'm the last one down. They've been waiting for me to arrive.

"Auntie Via, you had five more minutes, and I was going to jump on your bed 20 times to wake you up!" He sounds so disappointed, I laugh.

"Glad I missed that torture!"

"Who are you inviting?" he asks.

"Yeah, Big Sis, who?"

"Let me in on the list, Flower Bud!" Daddy adds.

"Your neighbors will be the most likely people who would gladly eat Lowcountry Boil instead of tradition!"

"That's actually a good thought!"

"Caleb, after we finish breakfast, we'll go on a neighborhood inviting journey. We won't let you down. We'll keep asking until we have three people saying yes. Is that okay with you?"

"Grand Pap, you won't be sorry! Inviting people is the best, right Mamma?"

"Yes, it is!" Meadow smiles at us all, and we eat her breakfast with gusto. She made us all pour over coffee to our individual liking, and I catch a whiff of Daddy's "little something" he adds in on holiday mornings.

We load them up with several rounds of goodbyes, and off they drive. Now, we really have to face our challenge.

"Let's go," Daddy begins to move toward the nearest neighbor's house with determination.

"Dad, let's talk about this! We can call them. One by one, we don't have to go there," Oakley tries.

Dad keeps bumping his walker over the uneven surface and walks on. We trade looks and step up beside him.

"I have regrets galore at this stage in my life. I'm not going to disappoint Caleb—end of discussion. Besides, the neighbors I'm heading for don't use their phones, but for emergencies. Mr. Mack Grant is the first one we'll ask."

Little girl Vinca complies, and adult Vinca seethes. I'm still in my PJs walking down the country lane with my Daddy pushing his walker and my brother in tow. We reserve our strength by keeping silent. There's nothing to say when Daddy has made his mind up. I do have my phone and can call 911 should that become necessary. We both spot a dirt drive up ahead about 50 feet. We both hope that's where the neighbor we are inviting lives.

"Stop!" Daddy commands.

"Plan B. Oakley, you stay here with me, as I will never survive the trip there and back home. Do you understand?"

"Dad, I'm not 10 years old, I..."

"Vinca, you will turn down that drive and walk up to the Grants' house. Now, they have a dog that is friendly but likes to bark. Ignore him, and he will ignore you. I trust you can handle a dinner invitation properly with all your experience in solving problems. Do your very best! Caleb is counting on us."

"What the heck?..."

One well-aimed stern look and many shallow breaths later, I sprint down the lane to the drive, rehearsing my invitation. I try out several versions in cadence with my running feet. My wonderful reverie stops as the friendly barking dog and I meet. He can look me eye to eye because he jumps at me and places his huge paws on each of my shoulders, the better to bark in my ears. It is impossible to ignore this dog.

"Down!" I command in my best leadership-team-manager-voice. To my utter amazement, he sits and crouches down to the driveway level.

"Good dog!" His tail thumps appreciation.

"Stay!" I add and walk up to the screened front porch. Amazingly, he is command-trained and does not move. This cold call in person is even more anxiety-producing than a phone call. Facing down my dad in his walker to refuse to obey his command is simply not an option.

Before I can let the fear take over, I rush up the steps and holler into the open door off the porch. That is perfectly acceptable in this part of the SC woods. It is actually considered neighborly and not intrusive at all.

"Hey, Mr. Grant! Can you hear me? It's Vinca Murray, Charlie's oldest, you know, from down the road?" I chatter as I hear him coming to the door.

"Well, well, look what we have here! Girl, I would know you anywhere. That streak in your hair done give you away. How are you? What you doing outchere? Yo daddy okay?" All one long sentence in the beautiful Sea Island language that sings like no other.

"He is great, Mr. Grant! In fact, he and my brother Oakley are waiting on the road for me to come back. They sent me over here to invite you and your family to come eat Thanksgiving with us. What you need to know is, it's not traditional, it's Lowcountry Boil!"

"Well, let me see. Let me see. I can't count on my family to follow through with the plans they make. Many a time I sit here waiting for them to come 'round for me, and it never happens. You know, I don't really care much for an old bird for dinner any day, but some shrimp, corn, and such, now that sounds like a feast. What time you plannin' on eatin'?"

"We don't have a set time, just come when you are ready. We'll eat when we get hungry. We caught the shrimp yesterday and made up the Lowcountry Boil last night, so all we need to do is warm it up. We made enough for sharing even before we knew we would be asked to share. Okay, see you later then!"

I shake his hand. He hugs me sideways, and off I go. One guest down, two more to ask. Mr. Grant calls the dog in, and I sprint back to the waiting force of Daddy and Oakley with no fear of a huge animal encounter.

"Well, that didn't take very long. Is he in or not?" Daddy asks.

"He's in! He said..." I try to give him the details as he raises his hand and voice to silence me cold.

"Stop. Listen, we don't have time for the story of the day."

"Okay, then." I make the zip my lips motion, and Oakley laughs until Daddy gives us his Tiger Eye.

"We need to invite Jacob Malone, one of my old fishing buddies. This invite'll have to be done over water in the johnboat. I think his college-age grandson might be there too, so that will finish out our obligation. Let's go!" He turns his walker around, and we march off into the next plan of action.

The walk back home reminds me of so many times we navigated this road in the past. Daddy moves deliberately and with little speed. We decide to head to the boat after a short pit stop, and soon are on the still water, puttering down the creek, breathing in cadence with the world. We wrapped a throw around Daddy's legs and had him sit on a flotation pillow. The Coast Guard or DNR rarely comes this far inland. We are safe with no fear of being fined for not wearing life jackets. His serene smile settles in the milky fall sunlight, his hat back on his head, a man and his boat in one accord.

As we pull up to the dock. Mr. Malone's college-age granddaughter, not his grandson, whom we have never met, is obviously home and obviously on the dock. She has a tangle of a mess with a fishing line and is attempting to straighten it out. She just looks at us. Her face, soft and angled at the same time, shines with beads of sweat from the effort. She wears her college swag well and looks as graceful as a ballerina on a football field.

"Grab the line!" Daddy yells.

"What?" College-girl answers, as Oakley motions for me to steer while he jumps skillfully on the dock and ties us off.

"Sheesh...Where's your granddad? You know, the man who pays for that fancy university you attend?" Daddy continues.

"He's inside. I'll get him, but please don't mention the mess I made of his fishing pole. I sort of let him think I knew what I was doing. I obviously don't," she rushes off and goes inside to get Mr. Jacob.

"What's up, Charlie? You have not come along to my dock in ages! Hello, Oakley. You've got to be Vinca, right? Have you met my granddaughter, Kyle? Kyle, this is Mr. Charlie, the best trout fisherman on this creek. These are two of his three kids, Oakley and Vinca."

We all say niceties and chat about nothing in particular until Daddy feels it's time for the invite.

"We're here on official business for my grandson, Caleb. He wants us to invite people over for Thanksgiving. Can you two come? We will be serving leftover Lowcountry Boil, shrimp caught yesterday by the same aforementioned boy. Come anytime. We will eat when we get hungry."

They look at each other and both break into laughter.

"You couldn't have come at a better time. I forgot to defrost the bird. It's hard as a brick and will probably be thawed enough to eat by Saturday. Sure, Kyle and I would love it. Have you got dessert? I do have a pie we picked up at the Farmer's Market yesterday. I'll send you a text when we set out your way."

"Great! We've got some ice cream, so we can go à la mode. You have no idea how much it means to me to help Caleb! Let's go, Oakley, lots to do, like take a nap, before all our company arrives."

When Daddy is ready to leave, he is ready to leave. We wave to our dinner guests and pull away from their dock.

We run the creek back home in contented silence. My thoughts merge in and out as the waterway, edged with the golden brown Spartina grass, takes me back and forward at the same time. The first males in my life, my father and my brother, and this water calls to my heart. I answer with a sigh as we pull up to our dock. I hop off the boat to tie up with all the muscle memory of years gone by.

We help Daddy get his walker situated for navigating the path into the house. I wonder if we are starting a new tradition masterminded by the youngest of the family, or if we are borrowing trouble. I wonder, will everybody lie?

Chapter 14
No Reply is Okay

Since we decided on leftovers, we really have little to do to prepare our Thanksgiving meal. Daddy goes to put his feet up for a bit. According to him, he never naps. He sits in his recliner, lying back and snoring, his feet up in the center of the house, but is not napping. Oakley and I set the kitchen right again after breakfast. We talk about nothing and everything. We make sure the table will meet approval and add some extra chairs to the screened porch.

"When do you think our guests will come over?" I ask Oakley.

"Knowing both of those men from the time I've been living here, I'd say they will come within an hour."

"Really? I'll be quick. I want to change into my company clothes for a proper Thanksgiving ambiance."

"That's a great idea. You've got time. Oh, they won't come empty-handed. They do get together and come here on some weekends. They like to play cards with Dad for old times' sake. I think they are all three lonely guys in many ways. They are good company for each other. I haven't seen them eat a lot; it's mostly liquids served. Are you going to be okay with that?"

"I'll try my best. I was hoping to talk with you about the woman and kitten in the park some more before they get here."

"Okay, by me. Go change, and we can sit out on the dock, so dad can rest and doesn't hear us."

After I change, we make our way to the dock. I fill him in on my latest encounter with the woman and her bizarre staring. He listens well, interrupting every now and then to comment and ask a question or two.

"I don't know what to think about all that other than to tell you to stay away from her."

"That's just it, I can't! I think about capturing the kitten and taking it to the vet. I know just how to make that happen. I've planned it with great detail. I wake up at 1 AM thinking about the whole situation."

"What are you going to do with another cat? What if your old Georgie girl hates it? What about the woman's reaction?"

"My sane mind knows all this, but that crazy part of me keeps planning the cat rescue and sees Georgie playing with and loving on the new arrival! The weirdest part is her piercing stare and the effect it has on me. I mean, I couldn't move my feet! Really, I was frozen."

"Via, you are not going to catch that kitten and ruin the woman's companion relationship! Her kitten could be a therapy cat. Let the whole thing go, okay? Don't make me have to come there and rescue you from a small white woman in a trench coat!"

As we laugh together, we hear the sound of a watercraft and the holler of a neighbor coming through the yard at the same time. I glance at my phone for the time, and Oakley is spot on; one hour has passed. As if on cue, Caleb sends us a text from Meadow's phone.

'Did you invite three people yet?'

'Yes! They are coming over right now, will send you pics soon.'

'happy face emoji'

Daddy and Mr. Grant are vocal and loud enough for their voices to reach us on the dock through the open kitchen window.

"Freddy, it's me, MG! Get your slow self outta the bed and outchere with the rest of us!"

"I hear you, MG, I really do! Come inside and help me with something..."

Oakley expertly ties up the Malones' boat just like our Pap taught him. I grab the pie from Kyle and help her climb onto our dock.

"Wait, please. Can I get one picture of us to send to Caleb? We have to prove to him we really invited three guests!"

"Sure, you two really clean up well. You both look ready for a photo shoot," he answers.

We stand in a line, and Oakley stretches his arm perfectly to capture us all in the shot. We plan to include the other two when we go inside.

"I'm sure glad for Caleb challenging you to do this, or we would have been eating sandwiches and pie today! Thank you," Mr. Malone laughs, and Kyle joins in.

"Will you take this pie up and check on things, Oakley? I thought I heard Daddy asking for Mr. Grant to help him with something. Kyle and I will catch up with you in a few minutes," I add, glancing at her to see if she is okay with that.

"Yeah, Grandad. I'll see you in a bit," she says and looks at me with a slight smile.

"I thought you might like to learn how to catch the boat line and tie it off at the dock. Has your granddad taken you fishing or out on the river yet?"

"Not yet, I just got here last night. He wants to, though, so maybe tomorrow. I feel so stupid not knowing how to do any of this stuff. I haven't been able to come visit him in a long time. You saw what I did to the fishing pole line, cord, string, or whatever you call that tangled mess I made."

"Yeah, I saw. So, let's start with the ins and outs of the boat and tie up the boat skills first. If there's time today, I'll help you a little with the fishing. But most granddads want to teach their grandkids themselves. It might hurt his pride if you know how to handle a fishing rod already."

We practice and talk, nothing serious, just college majors, what year she's in, her hobbies, my work, easy and gentle, safe topics. Oakley calls to us that the men are rumbling about being hungry, and we go inside to help arrange our feast. We unpack the leftovers when I see a pan of collard greens on the counter.

"Where did these come from? I haven't had any decent greens in a year!"

"I made 'em yesterday! Fresh from my garden with one frost on 'em. They'll be the sweetest, tenderest greens you ever put in yo' mouth, fo' sure," Mr. Grant informs us with a huge grin.

"You can have my share, too, Flower Bud. Your Ma tried to get me to eat those vile things the first time I ever set foot in this house. It was Thanksgiving then, too. No, wait, it was New Year's Day! If you eat them, she said, you will have lots of money. I took one small taste to make her happy, but I could not even swallow them! They also made me try Hoppin' John, that rice and cow pea dish. That's one food I could eat, and I enjoyed every bite. They bring good luck. They must have worked, because I married your mother later that year!"

"Good times, fo' sure, fo' sure."

"Kyle, you have to try those collards!"

"After that description, I can hardly wait," she says. I snap a quick shot of Daddy and Mr. Grant and send a text to Meadow's phone. We leave the guests and Daddy talking and laughing. We ask Kyle to give us a hand setting up for dinner.

Oakley and I arranged everything with her help. We use the dishes that have been in this house since before we were born. These are what our Momma called the good dishes. It was good that they all matched and none were ever dropped or broken! The edge of each plate has a circle of color that is repeated in shades of greens and blues. We set the table with placemats in fall colors and uncover some candles from the recesses of the pantry. Some high, some low, casting just the right amount of light as a centerpiece. Everything glistens and shines just right. Kyle asks if she can snip some flowers and cuttings from the yard if we have a tall, slender vase. I take a shot of the table to add to the photo collection.

We admire everything on the table, and the addition of the cuttings adds the final touches. We set up the food and made a buffet line in the kitchen. We know the table setting is perfect when the three men stop talking and just look at us and each other. When we are all seated, we grasp hands and bow our heads. Daddy asks a blessing over the food and us.

"Our Great and Generous God, we give you humble thanks for this feast and these wonderful neighbors to share it with. Bless all this and Caleb for his idea to make this a true Thanksgiving. Amen."

We raise our heads as we prepare our plates. All of us sit at the table and enjoy the feast and the neighbors. Oakley and I sip on wine while the older men hit the harder stuff. I mix a mocktail for Kyle, promising her wine in her senior year. We will make sure the boat runs with a sober driver, as well as driving Mr. Grant home if need be. Georgie hangs out under the table, and all three men sneak her shrimp. I keep my mouth shut.

We bring out the pie, rich and flaky, with the juices bubbling between the edges of the crust. We top off each slice à la mode with the rich vanilla ice cream.

"This is about the nicest Thanksgiving I've had in a long time. Caleb must be one smart kid!" Mr. Grant adds.

"To Caleb!" Daddy adds as we raise our glasses and repeat the sentiments. The three men decide to start their favorite card game, and the three of us youngsters clean up and move out to sit on the porch and watch the sunset.

"Can we get back home in the dark on that little boat?" Kyle asks.

"Yes, if you have a light. But, I will taxi you and your granddad with my boat if the night is not too cold. Then I'll come back and drive Mr. Grant home in the car. It could be a cold night for the Lowcountry, and a boat ride can be brutally chilly with the humidity and wind. You and your granddad don't have warm enough jackets. I can pick him up whenever he's ready to come and get the boat and take it back. If you're too tired before he's ready to go, you can stay over in Meadow's room if you want to, or I'll run you home. I went to high school with your mom. She was a good friend to me! I can pay her back in a small way by taking care of you! So, just relax and enjoy with no worries," Oakley replies.

We pull out the Domino set and begin our own game with lots of laughter and strategies all around. Kyle fits in like a younger sister, and the men play on.

Around ten, Daddy pushes back from the table and pulls his walker close.

"Okay, comrades, time to go! Happy Thanksgiving, and all that! Good night to you! You have worn this old man out! Oakley, drive these dinner guests home." They all laugh and act offended and begin moving to the door.

"I'll drive! It's really too late and too cold to take the boat. My car is the easiest to pull out, and Oakley, you can get Daddy settled with his routine while I'm gone. Mr. Malone, we'll get your boat to you tomorrow. Won't take me 15 minutes!"

Once all are in my car and settled, we make the drop-offs, and I'm on the way back home. So many memories hiding in my deepest regrets tie up with my heart and soul angst. No regrets this year as we listened to Caleb.

We say our good nights. I decide I will stay tomorrow and see if Daddy will go through another stack of photos and help them with things around the house. Wonder where the CW and her flashing cat spent their Thanksgiving? I wonder if Tony's fried turkey was a success. I dare myself to text him..

'Hope your turkey turned out well. My Thanksgiving was with three old men friends, one new college girl, and my brother. Not what

I expected, but wonderful. Happy Thanksgiving!' Before I can talk myself out of it, I hit send.

I put my phone down, anticipating nothing. No reply is okay. Any reply is okay. Okay is where I am right now. Protected from any more lies, potential for lies, and lack of ability to face truth, which equals more lies anyway you slice it.

I brush my teeth in my PJs, my wild hair free all around my shoulders. I hear the CW whisper in that hollow, sharp way she has in my ear, "Everybody lies."

Chapter 15
An Idea Worth Exploring

I told the CW to shut up, put my phone on do not disturb, opened my window a little wider, and let the night air in. I sleep surrounded by memories that don't invade, wrapped in love that's not the smothering kind, but love that knows when to back off and when to come in close, a place of peace. I sleep the best sleep in a long time, probably resulting from the utter exhaustion of being on my best behavior for the past 24 hours.

I enjoy the predawn concert of the barred owls calling to each other. The deep sounds echo and carry over the tree tops as the call and responses cascade back and forth. Soon, the room begins to lighten, and I can see the familiar furniture sharpen and clarify in my eyesight. Georgie paws my arm, more than ready for her breakfast.

I shuffle, and she sprints to the kitchen. I feed her and make coffee, staring out the back at the still water, watching a mullet jump in leaps across the surface, sending out rings before submerging again.

"What adventures will this day bring?" I ask Georgie. She wraps herself around my legs in a figure eight and purrs, probably thinking about the shrimp she ate and how this place is cat perfection.

We move out to the porch, and I grab the roomy rocker. Georgie loves to be rocked, and I'm happy to comply as I sip, rock, and continue a conversation only a cat can hear. I'm feeling a sense of action, a pull to do something. I fight the urge to act because it feels so good to be able to relax and sit with my cat in my family home and just be. When was the last time I did this? My phone has not buzzed all morning! Usually by this time, I have a rush of texts and emails to attend to from office stuff, mostly. Before I can marvel anymore, I realize it is still set on do not disturb. As I switch the settings, I see I have 14 texts and even more emails.

"Well, it was nice while it lasted, right, Georgie?"

I decide to only read the texts from family, and let the others go. Caleb loves the pictures and sends one of Jonathan and him smiling, each holding a turkey leg. That evokes feelings I didn't know I'd have for my little man nephew and his dad time. As I am sorting, I see a reply from Tony. He sent me a picture of his turkey! And let me know it was a good Thanksgiving with a reminder that I don't owe him anything, but if I want an idea, he loves to fish. I can wait to reply, or I can send a safe emoji like a thumbs up, not a commitment, just 'I like that you love to fish'. I wait for now because I feel my coffee clenching in my belly at the thought of him coming out here to fish. That sounds too personal and too "meet this guy" father and brother.

"Whoa, you scared me! I almost dropped my phone in the water! Make some noise when you walk up to a distracted person!"

"Sorry, Sis! I always had the ability to scare you, didn't I? Just came out to ask you if you want some breakfast? Daddy's not up yet. I looked in on him and made sure his chest was rising and falling. I think he's just worn out from yesterday. That is the farthest he has walked in forever, and the longest day he spent drinking, smoking, card playing, and eating."

"Are you sure he's okay? Should we wait on him?"

"I'm sure. And no, he would want us to eat. I have everything to make chocolate chip waffles. I thought Caleb might like those, or at least be a great excuse for me to eat some. I think we have bacon, too. Maybe 15 minutes?"

"I shouldn't, but I will!"

"You sit out here and enjoy. I'll cook, and you can clean. We can talk about the rest of the day over breakfast."

When was the last time I cooked a decadent breakfast? This would be a real treat. I start scrolling through my news feed and social media, exactly what I swore I would not do. I stop before I get too far in and just sit. There is nothing on here that can't wait one more day. If I leave tomorrow, I can get some of my Christmas decorations up.

Sometimes, a dolphin will randomly take a swim alone or with a buddy or a calf to feed on the mullet I saw jumping earlier. They herd the fish in teams and force them to swim on the sand at the ocean or the mud at the marsh. When they get them all in a swirling, shimmering frenzy, they feed by speed swimming into the fish, mouths wide open, filling themselves up with the swirling mass of mullet. They are fascinating to watch, and the coast of South Carolina is the only place where all the conditions are right for this type of feeding. The pshhing of air released from the blowhole as they break the water surface is the first warning that a dolphin is nearby. They swim in the most graceful undulations, up and under, submerge and rise: some of nature's most beautiful creatures. My grandparents called them porpoises, true to their Lowcountry heritage. I hear Oakley call to me as I put my phone in my pocket and enjoy the feast he has made.

"So, what do you want to do today after we run Mr. Malone's boat back to his dock? You can follow me in the johnboat. We can fish again, throw the cast net? Or, maybe you need a lazy day just to read? I can drag out the hammock for you and get it set up on the porch. Even if it rains, you can still enjoy."

"That sounds perfect. The hammock, I mean. I'm just realizing how long it has been since I really relaxed. When I'm in my condo, I find a million things I have to do. Here, it is easier to just let it go. Mostly because I see how much you and Daddy have under control. You really are taking great care of him, and it looks like yourself, too. Are you seeing anyone? Do you even have a chance to get out?"

"Yes, I get out. Those two old men, as you call them, make me! They take turns coming over to sit with Daddy, so I can get a few hours away by myself. A group of us from my Clemson days meet in Charleston on a regular basis to toast to old times and have dinner. It's a good mix of singles and couples, just great friends and good company. I have dinner or occasionally cook for a female friend here, but we are treading water right now, neither of us ready to actually swim. Don't want to say any more, or tell you her name, so don't even ask! I know where I'm needed right now, and anything more time-consuming or serious would not fit into my life or Daddy's."

"Do you think he's getting worse?"

"In some ways. He seems more forgetful and confused at times, which is hard to take. You know how intelligent he is and up to date. He stopped watching all TV except for sports because he doesn't understand the commercials for the new products, saying they make no sense to him."

We both chuckle in that sad way when the humor hurts, but is so true. We linger over the food, coffee, and company, letting the morning stretch out. Around 11, the sound of Daddy's walker wheels rolling on the hardwood can be heard.

"Where are my good-for-nothing oldest two? Can't a father get a fresh coffee around here? Don't suppose you saved any of that food for me?" We both laugh and meet him in the kitchen.

"I'll get Daddy set up and clean the dishes if you get that hammock ready for me!" I pour fresh batter into the waffle iron and get him his favorite mug down, the one Caleb's school sold as a fundraiser with artwork by the students. Caleb drew a childhood version of a pink shrimp. None of us told him they are only pink when they have been cooked! Best Grand Pap, written under the drawing, completes the scene.

"So, going to have some hammock time? Yes, indeed, your Momma and I loved our hammock time. Even after all this time, I can remember it like it was yesterday, even if I have no idea what day of the week it is!"

I take my time gathering up a stack of things I brought with me to read. I grab the soft throw I gave Daddy last Christmas and park myself in the best spot ever. The hammock, a true Pawley's Island gem, is the epitome of comfort. This one has a cover that ties on and a long rolling pillow, great for neck support. Soon, I settle in and hold the edge still so Georgie can jump in. We sway gently back and forth with my left foot on the floor, providing just enough force to keep us moving in a relaxing rhythm. I read for a few hours, oblivious to the goings on around me. I hear an occasional murmur or shout from inside as the men of the house watch football and cheer on or jeer at their teams. I pull up my leg and let myself fall into the best afternoon nap I can manage with a warm cat, a swaying cradle, and all the comforts of home.

As I return to reality, I think about what Oakley shared and go to find him.

"Look, I know your friends who couldn't go to what we love to call The Palmetto Bowl are here in Charleston for the weekend. Why don't you meet them? I'll be here with Daddy, and we will be fine, just fine."

He stares at me for a moment before he responds.

"Yes! I wasn't going to meet them and had made up my mind that I would be okay with that. But now that we have been talking about all of this, I think I'll go. More than that, I need to go. Thanks, Sis." He hugs me as he sets up Daddy's meds and rushes away to get ready to go out.

"Just you and me, Flower Bud! Looks like Oakley wants to get away for a bit. We'll be fine. I'm planning on a quiet evening. All that visiting and talking, laughing, and playing the great host wears a man down. I'm down for sure. Not bad, just know I need a good night's sleep.

Maybe we can watch one of those movies, or I suppose I can try to ID some more of the old photos."

"Daddy, I'm not going to force you, but I really would like to try if you feel like it. If we go through a few stacks every time I come, we can get them all done without too much heartache. Just in case, I'll look for something you might like to watch with me."

We tell Oakley to have fun and set ourselves up with a tray of various cheeses, deli meat, crackers, and wine for me, a small glass of cheer for him. We snack with easy conversation. I'm thankful he doesn't ask me much about my love life or if I will ever get serious about a man again. I do tell him about the ticket, embellishing the story to make him laugh and to make myself feel better, too. I even added the part about Meadow's connection with Tony and his ability to take care of the problem.

"It pays to have friends in many places. Don't discount anyone. You never know who might be your boss one day or offer you a favor when you least expect it. On the other hand, don't think too highly of yourself or that you can't offer to give someone else a hand up."

Smiling, as I have heard those words verbatim all my life, in fact, I could have recited them with him. Instead, I reply, "I'll keep all of that in mind, Daddy. All of it."

"Help me take these awful pills! I need you to open up the containers. They're all lined up in order already. I'm a party pooper this evening! I'm just tired, so no worries."

I help him and see that he is headed to complete his routine and settle in. I stand in the hallway as he undresses by sitting on the side of the bed. He picks up his legs and lifts them onto the bed, and scoots into a comfortable spot. I walk in and plant a kiss on his forehead.

"Love you, Daddy! This has been a nice visit."

"You, too, Flower Bud. Yes, it has. Turn that lamp off, if you will, and go back to your relaxing. Oakley usually comes in around 11."

I follow his directions and wander out to the screened porch again. A slow, gentle rainfall hits the tin porch roof, the best white noise ever. I feel the damp edge of the hammock and decide to stretch out on the couch instead with a throw and fall back into my book. As soon as Georgie sees me with the throw and book, she gets ready to curl up beside me. The house settles, the ticking clock competing with the rainfall, the curtains blowing against the screen. I easily identify all the familiar and new sounds, content and grateful to escape into my book.

My phone buzzes me back to reality. I see Oakley has texted that he's on the way. I give up resisting the other texts and see that I never answered Tony further on the fishing. Feeling some false bravado, I try several attempts to reply and then hit delete.

'Fishing it is. Just know that I was born with a pole in my hands.'...Too corny and clichéd.

'LOL I can try the fishing challenge.'...Too poor, dumb me.

'That's an idea worth exploring.'... Just right, and I send it.

He sends back a thumbs-up.

I go on autopilot, waiting for Oakley to come in. Too tired to read any more, watch anything, or fall asleep yet, I scroll through all my favorite sites. From skimming posts to adding a comment here and there, I absentmindedly glance at a few more when my fingers stop. I stare at the photo of a woman who was found unconscious in the town square of Summerville. It is my Crazy Woman!

I would know that face anywhere. Those eyes are ingrained in my mind. What the heck? She was found, with no ID, taken to the Tricare Hospital, and no one has any idea who she is. The photo has been shared over and over, with people posting asking for anyone who knows her to come forward. She has been there since Tuesday. The latest post says she cannot stay in the hospital any longer and will be released to the proper authorities, who will help her find shelter and hopefully her family.

My heart pounds. I kept thinking of her, didn't I? I should have known something was wrong. I can't help but think of her as my CW. What is that poor kitten doing for shelter now that its deep pocket is missing? Oh, what a mess. I need to call this number right away. Better yet, I've got to go home and ID this woman.

Just as I am punching in the number, Oakley comes in the door. He looks at me sitting up with a horrified face and plops down on the sofa.

"What's happening, Via? You look ready to jump out the window?"

"You won't believe what's happening, and I was just calling the Summerville PD right before you walked in the door. Before you freak out, all family members are safe! But this is crazy, just ridiculous!"

"Wait. Wait, and slow down. Why do you need the Summerville PD? What's happened?"

I take a few breaths and condense the latest happening with the CW into a story he can follow without too many confusing details and irrelevant facts.

"See, why I need to call right now! You know how much I hate cold calls, so don't even try to stop me. This woman needs ID, and I may very well be the only person she has talked to in the past month." I start to hit the call button when he grabs my hand.

"Vinca, stop! Calling this woman "CW" is not going to fly as an ID. You don't know anything about her identity. No name, no address. The best you can tell them is that you saw her, where she was, and where she went, as far as you could tell. You can't ID her any more than I can!"

"What about that poor kitten? Oakley, I've got to do something!"

He pours us both a glass of wine, and we talk through all the options that make the most sense. We agree she is in a safe place for now, and there is no reason this call can't wait until the morning. I tell him I agree and set off to bed, yawning as I go. Once in my room, I pull out clothes for tomorrow and pack everything else as quietly as I can. I set my alarm for 5:00 AM and let Georgie know her Cat Spa Vaca is as good as done. We aren't going to call. That is the truth. We're going straight to the Summerville PD. I'll text Tony before we pull out and ask him to meet us there. Perfect example of who you know matters. Georgie will be fine in her crate long enough for me to ID the CW. After that, I will find the kitten.

Chapter 16
Don't Panic!

I manage to call up my teen days and leave the house in complete silence, even with a cat in a crate and my rolling bag. I take a chance that Tony is a morning person and send off a text at 5:20 AM.

'Good morning'... maybe he is not a morning person. Delete.

'Apologies for this early text. I need advice. Which means, I'll owe you two. The unidentified woman who is in the hospital... I know her. Can you tell me the next steps? I'm leaving Adams Run now.'

I wait to see if the three dots appear. Nothing. I guess he's not a morning person after all. I put my phone on the passenger seat and pull out on the road before Oakley or Daddy wakes up.

All the rest of the ride, I feel an urgency that is troubling. Oakley is right. I don't know this woman's name or address, but I do feel an obligation to her and her kitten. Oh, what has happened to that feline? At least I can let her know I will try to locate the cat. That I can do. Even if I just let CW know I am looking for her cat, that might help her in some weird way. I ask Siri to call Meadow.

"Don't panic! Everyone is okay."

"Geez, Via, my heart stopped! Whatever is making you call me this early better be good," she whispers into her phone, trying not to awaken Caleb.

"I need your wisdom and your understanding, okay? No judging, just listen."

"Now, I'm really worried."

"Meadow, that crazy woman I told you about, she is in TriCare as a Jane Doe!"

"Okay..."

"I want to help her. I feel an overwhelming need to help her."

"Vinca, you don't know her. She has said the same two words to you every time you have tried to interact with her. Clearly, she's not stable. Just how are you planning to do this?"

"Momma, is that Auntie V?"

Great, Caleb is awake all because of me.

"Yes, Buddy. Go ahead and get up. You can have free time for a bit while I finish talking, okay?"

"Tell him I send love and hugs."

"Hold on a sec," I hear her mumbling with him, and some shuffling of bedclothes and a door closing.

"Go on, Via. What are you planning to do? Where are you right now, anyway?"

"I'm in the car on the way back, talking to you, because I want to drive straight to TriCare and get her out of there! So I called you. You know, for wisdom. And support..."

"You left this early? Wait, you didn't even say goodbye, did you?"

"Yes, but... not in person. I left a note. Look, what should I do? You've got to help me out here!"

"First of all, I doubt TriCare will let you see her. How did you find out about this?"

"I saw it on my news feed last night. Apparently, someone took a photo of her when she was found unconscious and posted it on all platforms to see if anyone would come forward with an ID. No one has. I can't stop thinking about that poor kitten and CW."

"Wait, don't they usually have a tip line people can call to give information? Putting you on speaker so I can look. Yes, there's a number!"

"Great, I guess I was so caught up in the horror of the story, I skipped right over that part. I'm about 20 minutes away. Do you mind if I come over and call with you there? You know how I hate to make cold calls. That gives me time to think about what to say."

"Sure, I'll put some coffee on and pull out some kind of breakfast. You know this is going to be a dead end, right? I mean, your intelligent rational mind has to know that, right?"

"Maybe not. Maybe all she needs is to know I'm looking for her cat. Maybe that will trigger something for her. What do hospitals do with unidentified people when they release them?"

"I'll see what I can find out. Try to focus on getting here safely, and I'll do a little research."

"Oh, I sent a text to Tony as soon as I got in the car. I think he might be a good source of information."

"Oh, you did, did you? Is that the only reason?" she laughs. I'm not in the mood.

"Cut it, Meadow. This is not funny to me!"

"Okay, okay-sorry to offend you. See you soon."

I decide to take Georgie home. As soon as I pull up in my driveway, Oakley calls. I don't answer. He calls twice more and texts.

'I need to know that you're ok.'

'I'm ok. With Meadow. Will call later.'

I drop Georgie in the entryway of the condo and open the door of the crate. She rushes out straight to her feeding area and meows in the obviously starving way of cats. I quickly feed her and leave water.

Drive time was quick, with this being a holiday weekend, and I find myself thinking about Tony. Of course, I did stalk social media to look at his photos with Meadow, so I could jog my memory of what he looked like when he offered to help with my problem. He is brown in all combinations: 1. hair that is wavy and short, 2. eyes that are deep and long-lashed, 3. skin that says fresh air and sunshine. Why did I not remember all this? Anyway, maybe he will see my text sometime today.

When I pull up at Meadow's house, I'm convinced that the CW's crazy is contagious. My little sister lets me know she's talked to Oakley and assured him she won't let me do anything dangerous.

We sit together on the porch swing. I punch in the info line number on my phone. I don't put it on speaker. I'm trying to keep Caleb from hearing any of this.

"Information tip-line. How can I help you?"

"Yes, my name is Vinca Murray."

"Ma'am, this tip-line is anonymous. No need to give any personal information."

"Okay. Forget that. I'm calling because I have information on Jane Doe, who was found unconscious and is in TriCare."

"Go on."

"She is in the town square area a lot in the afternoon. She has a very distinct odor about her of unwashed hair. She has a small orange tabby she lets into the pocket of her trench coat. She wears that thing in all sorts of weather." As I talk, I begin to accept how little I really do know.

"Is there anything else you can add?"

"She has said the same two words to me all of the times I have seen her."

"What would those words be?"

" 'Everybody lies.' "

Pause.

"What is her name? How old is she? Where does she live?"

"I have no idea. I told you all I have. Look, I want to let her know I'm going to find her cat. And take care of it until she can. Can you get that message to her?"

"No, I can only take your information. I understand you are concerned. Thank you for your input." Click.

"Well, I think you did all you could do."

"I don't know! Do you and Caleb want to help me find the kitten? It usually hangs around between my office and Azalea Park. I brought some of Georgie's food just in case. I really want to find a way to let her know I'm looking and willing to care for the cat. Did you find out anything else?"

"If she is homeless, there are laws that provide shelter for a limited time until she can leave. But, with her communication issues, it seems like she is experiencing some cognitive problems as well. I'm not sure what happens then."

As the morning passes, the three of us look all over for the kitten. We stop at every place I saw that little rascal. I even leave some food under the tree roots where I first met the CW.

I've talked to Oakley and thanked him for a great Thanksgiving. As we near lunch time, I see a burly man with all that is brown, walking toward us.

"Meadow, you did not! Please, tell me you did not call Tony."

She laughs—no denial or confirmation. Caleb runs up the walkway to high-five Officer Garcia.

"Looks like you haven't found the kitten yet?" He smiles. I find myself noticing how white and straight his teeth are balanced against that strong brown jaw and those full lips. What am I doing?

"Uh, no kitty yet. How did you know we were here?" I ask. Did I just say "kitty" like a child?

"Meadow let me know what you were up to. I'm on call today, so I have to stay nearby. I took a chance you might be in the area."

"Oh. Just so long as I don't owe you two times!" I try to laugh off some of my anxiety and obsession with finding this small feline.

"Not at all. In fact, you don't even owe me one time, but I would like you to consider that fishing idea," he replies with a just right not too cocky and not too shy balance. I glance at Meadow, and she grins from ear to ear. Tony and I are at it again. What can I even say?

"Right now, all I can think about is that small orange tabby and its owner, Jane Doe."

"Yeah, I get that. I hear you want to try to let her know you're looking for the cat?"

"Yes! I'm thinking of going to TriCare and visiting her just to tell her. Do you think that would even be possible? Will I be able to get in? How will I find out what room she's in if I don't even know her name?"

"If you go during visiting hours, you won't have any trouble getting into the hospital. Not sure if you can ask to visit Jane Doe, but I can probably find out. Do you know the extent of her illness or injuries?"

"No, all the post shows is that she was found unconscious. From my interactions with her, I'd guess she might have fallen or been dehydrated. She seemed to be experiencing homelessness, but she could have a home, but likes to wander."

"We could ask Nurse Robbins," Caleb interjects. All three of us stop and take in what he says.

"She works at TriCare on the weekends sometimes and on some holidays. You know her, Mom, she's my school nurse. She called you when I threw up all over the desk in kindergarten!"

"Caleb, that's a good idea! Might be even better than Auntie Via going to visit and getting escorted out of the hospital for stalking a Jane Doe," Meadow adds.

My phone and Meadow's buzz at the same time. We both look at the text.

'Dad fell. On the way to the Ashley Towers Medical Center ED behind the EMS. Will update ASAP.'

Tony offers to look after Caleb so Meadow and I can ride together. We sprint back towards our vehicles. The feral cat and Jane Doe vanish from my thoughts for now. What was Daddy doing? Where did he fall? I take a chance and call Oakley on the way. He does not answer. Meadow sends him a text.

'We are on the way. Praying. Love you!'

Chapter 17
Pull it Together

D addy lies so still and pale. Monitors whirl a cacophony of discord around the cubicle. He is sedated. The three of us stand around the bed, praying silently, waiting for a room to come open. We've never been a family that prays aloud except at holidays over a meal. Momma taught us the best way to pray was private time with God, where you can bare your heart of hearts. We're connected in this silent prayer time. We wait for the answers we may not want, to fight it out with the answers we do want. All the while wondering what will happen? What is God's will?

He breathes shallow breaths and his nurse, Shane, comes in to check his vitals.

"He has the best team of caregivers in the state working for him," Shane assures us. "A room should be ready in an hour or so. Doctor Coleman will be in before then to help you understand what the test results show. Can I get anything for you?"

"Thank you, we can manage," Oakley replies.

Concerned that Daddy can somehow hear us, we whisper.

"I didn't hear a sound. I thought Daddy was sleeping late, like he did yesterday, so I just let him sleep until after 9. I was mad at you, Via, for leaving and chasing after that woman and her cat. I walked out on the dock to calm down. When I went in to check on him, he wasn't in his bed, or even his room. I found him on the bathroom floor! There was blood all over his face. His ankle was all twisted." He can't hold back the tears any longer, and we squeeze his hands even tighter.

"I'm so sorry about all of this! Anyway, I called 911. That was the longest 10 minutes of my life. I kept talking to him like he could hear me. I wanted him to know he wasn't alone. They made me stay in the waiting room when I got here. Nurse Shane let me know that most of the bleeding came from the cut on his head when he hit the floor. His ankle is broken. They are running more tests to help them understand what else might be going on. I feel awful. I got so mad, I didn't even check on him!"

"Oakley, stop. Right now, just stop. This was an accident. This was no one's fault. You need to pull it together and know we need to be strong for Daddy and each other!" Meadow tells him.

"Anyway, I share in your guilt! If I hadn't caused you to get so angry at my obsession with the woman and her cat, none of this would have happened. Just know, I am so sorry!" I add.

"You two! Put all that away. We need to be a positive force for Daddy and each other. If this is not helping, then why would we go there?" Meadow is right.

We each revert to silence and sit in the room watching the man who raised us. Not knowing the details of the present moment, my mind becomes crystal clear with the memories. The three of us with Daddy in this same hospital when Momma fought the cancer. The way we leaned on Daddy. The way we now must lean on each other.

How do we do this? One minute I'm saving a cat and a crazy woman, the next I'm watching my last living parent in limbo. As much as I knew this would happen one day, I'm not ready for it now. One day, Caleb was going to be in college, not a 6-year-old.

"Meadow, have you checked on Caleb?"

"Yes, Tony says he's fine. He told Caleb Grand Pap is sick, and we don't know yet what is wrong. He stayed with him until Autumn got home, and she took over. He said to tell you he will call Nurse Robbins."

"That's really the last thing on my mind, but I appreciate that he volunteered to do that."

Dr. Coleman walks into the cubicle. We all stand up as if on cue.

"Hi, I'm Dr. Coleman, the hospitalist on duty. Are you Mr. Murray's family?"

"Yes, we are! All three of us are his biological children from the same gene pool. Our mother was black. Amazing how we turned out, one mixed, one white, one black!" I mutter, so used to the startled looks on people's faces when we are together with my mixture, Oakley's whiteness, and Meadow's blackness.

"I see. Your dad will be moved upstairs to the PICU soon. We are still waiting on some more test results to confirm, but he may have had a minor stroke. He will need to do just what he is doing: rest. He's getting fluids through IV. Do you have any questions?"

We look at each other and shake our heads. What will the next steps be? How will we manage? How can I fix this? All I can hear is a minor stroke.

Chapter 18
Leading a Double Life

The three of us survive the next few days in a blur of driving to the hospital and back home. Daddy continues to need to be in the PICU. He did have a minor stroke. He can talk and use his left hand. His "good" leg is motionless, stabilized in a boot. He can't use the walker as he did before. The staff assures us their goal is to move him to a regular room as soon as possible and start him on PT, OT, and a plan to release him from the hospital.

He's in and out between clarity and confusion. When he's speaking, he's Dr. Murray again with patients to see and meds to dispense. Meadow suggests that on Sunday, we make some sort of schedule, so we don't all have to be there at the same time. Oakley agrees to take the day hours, and Meadow and I split the weeknights. The feeling of helplessness sneaks up on me like a nagging hangnail. I, for once, will be glad to have my job responsibilities to take my mind off Daddy's failing health. He can't walk. He can't stay in the present time.

I let my boss know I'll be at work for at least part of the day on Monday. She assures me I can have all the time I need. The evening spent with Georgie on my lap, watching some old favorites, allows me to lose myself in the plot line, so I don't have to think about this anymore. Utter exhaustion, like a weighted blanket I'm forced to drag around, sends me to a deep sleep for a few hours. I wake up fully clothed and twisted into a knot at 3 AM. Immediately, I go into problem-solving mode, my mind buzzes with one solution knocked out by another that all add up to ones that won't work. I give up trying to catch any more rest and take the longest, hottest shower I can stand. Georgie's meow for food brings me back to reality, and I step out to take care of her. While my coffee brews, I check my phone, which is right where I left it last night. I see a text from Tony.

'So sorry to hear about your dad and all that you and your family must be going through. Keeping you in my thoughts and prayers. Still looking for the kitten.'

Sad heart emoji because I have no words right now.

By the time I pull up at the office lot, the sun's starting to rise. My head is still in a fog of not enough sleep. With the 3 AM committee meeting in my head, the no-sleep brain fog lingers. I walk to the coffee shop on the square, thinking maybe a coffee and breakfast treat will help. Once I have my containers all secure in their carrier, I step out into the foggy morning as gray and listless as I feel right now. I stop by my car to grab my work bag from the back seat. I see the flash of orange that I have not been willing to admit that I've been looking for. I stop reaching and freeze in place, making all the friendly cat soothing sounds I know so well. I break off a piece of my breakfast and drop the crumbs on the pavement. I watch as the little-bit kitten stalks the food. Crouched down and ready to pounce, it jumps and nibbles. Waits and nibbles up the rest. Lifting its head, it looks at me as if to ask for more with a weak mew and pleading green eyes. I break off some more, and it sits down to eat. Before I process my next move, I have reached out my hand and grabbed the unsuspecting feline by the nape of the neck. It just dangles, purring and relaxed, and I can see "it" is a "he".

"Well, you rascal. I've finally got you. Now, is a terrible time for sure. Oh crap, you are covered with fleas! And who knows what else. I don't have anything with me that will help you right now! We're going to get in the car, and I'm going to come up with a solution! How does that sound to you?"

I wrap Rascal in a beach towel I keep in the trunk because I never know when I might need it, right? I have rolled him up like a burrito with just his head sticking out. That ought to keep most of the fleas contained, and me and my car interior safe. A flea, as if in defiance of my plan, scoots along his face into his right ear. I can't even take him to my condo like this!

"Okay, you! I'm going to sip my coffee, and we can share my treat while I try to sort this out. I need you to stay in that wrap and eat. You might weigh 2 pounds at best! I can see how hungry you are. By the way, I have no idea what the CW calls you, so I changed your name to Rascal." I keep the conversation going and pour some water into the lid of my water bottle and position him so he can lap up the liquid.

I text my boss that I'll be late for work. I call my vet and leave a message on their voicemail. I'm on my way with a male kitten malnourished and flea-infested.

I think about texting Tony, but I don't.

We pull up at the vet's. Rascal is still secure in his burrito beach towel. The receptionist lets me in.

"Got your message. The first thing we want to do is a flea treatment. Can he stay here for a few hours?"

"That would be great! Look, I found him. I don't own him. I believe he's feral. I named him Rascal. I can pay the bill, but I may need to have a payment plan. My Dad is in the PICU..." I start to cry. Really cry. All the pent-up bravado has left, and I'm a wreck in the vet waiting room with a flea-infested cat wrapped in a beach towel.

"Of course, Ms. Murray, so sorry to hear about your dad. I'll let you know how things are going in a few hours. One less thing to think about today. This little Rascal is lucky you found him!" She takes him from me, passes me a handful of tissues, and walks him back to the examining room, leaving me alone in the waiting room trying to regain my composure.

I decide to leave without waiting for her to return so I can avoid the details I'm not ready to discuss and get back to the office. Wait, I need to have some supplies for this animal if I'm going to care for him just for the time the CW, aka Jane Doe, is in the hospital. Which I don't even know is true with all the other goings on in my life right now. Maybe I will text Tony after I take a short trip to the closest store for the kitten's needs.

I go with a purpose, determined not to take too long. I grab a handheld basket to force myself to shop with reason. I select some kitten recommended food, a food and water bowl combo, a small carrier, and one toy, just one. I rush through the self-checkout and am back in my car before I realize I did not get any flea treatment for me or the interior of the vehicle. I'll know soon enough if that is needed. I drive back to work, desperate for something normal to focus on. How ironic I consider my work, with all its drama, normal today.

When I walk upstairs to my office space, I repeat I need normal. I need a plain, normal day. I will myself to take all that's going through my mind and compartmentalize. I put the situation with Daddy in the "wait" compartment, as Oakley is with him and will update if necessary. Meadow offered to take the visit tonight. That is one less thing on me today as I now have a feral cat, likely a huge vet bill pending, and a promise to Jane Doe I may not ever get to say to her. I must stop this line of thought. The tears start to pool up again. Maybe this was a mistake after all.

"Hey, Ms. V, whatever you need today, just ask, okay?" Clacinda greets me with a hug, and I'm so grateful. I dab at my face and sniff, pulling myself back together.

"Thanks so much. Right now, I need a normal workday. Can we make that happen?"

"Really? Does that ever happen around here?" We both laugh a little.

"You've got it! I'll be your assistant today and handle things as best I can without consulting you. I'll keep a list of what's urgent and what can wait. You can fully focus on our new client and come up with a plan for us to implement in case you need some time off later in the week."

"Thank you. That sounds perfect." She hugs me again and moves to her cubicle. I see an email come through to everyone with what she just proposed. I open the file on the new client and put all my mind on her company profile and how we can solve her marketing issues and income flow. I'm surprised two hours have passed when my phone buzzes. I see the vet's number on my caller ID.

"Ms. Murray, this is Shelia from Like Our Own Vet Clinic. I have an update on Rascal. He's had a complete round of flea treatment and a thorough exam. He does appear to be feral but somewhat socialized. His paw pads are rough, and he is malnourished. He needs to be fed a high-calorie diet and given some time to fatten up. When can you come and get him?"

"Thank you. That is good news, right? I'm at work and was hoping to stay a few more hours. I can work through lunch and leave early, around 3:00, if that works?"

"We're not busy right now, and he's in a crate sleeping. If we get really busy, I may have to have you come sooner than that. Dr. Johnson will work with you on the payment of the bill. She knows you are a reliable animal parent from your care of Georgie."

I let my boss know I'll be leaving by three. Oakley sends a group text to let us know Daddy is no worse or better than he was yesterday. He put a notepad in the room, so we can all write down what the doctor says. The next shift of the three of us can read it and ask any questions later. While I have my phone in my hand, I text Tony.

'Daddy is stable but no change. BTW, I found the kitten.' The flutter of excitement at seeing the three dots of him replying surprises me.

'Hang in there! Glad to tell you, Nurse Robbins may be able to let Jane Doe know you found the cat.'

'That makes me feel better in a weird way. Gotta go pick his flea-free self from my vet and probably take out a small loan to pay the bill.'

Thumbs up emoji.

I try not to think about what Georgie will do with this Rascal male cat as I pull up to the vet. I pay what I can on the bill and grab the bag full of his treatments for relief from a malnourished life. He is very still in the carrier until I start the car. Now, I meet the howling version of Rascal. I turn up the music. He turns up the howl. We play this game twice more, and I give up. I try singing to him any random song I can. He pauses in the howling and seems to listen. This is the longest twenty-minute ride ever. Thankfully, the traffic is light at this time of day. I imagine what torture I would have endured stuck bumper to bumper with that caterwauling noise.

I pick up all his menagerie of items, spot the towel, and drop it in the dumpster, wishing I had noticed it at the vets. I make a mental note to research how to de-flea a car. I talk to him as we walk up to the condo. He's very agreeable while I'm in motion. When I put down the crate to unlock the door, he warms up his vocal cords again. I hear Georgie answering back. He raises his small cat back in the aggressive stance of all felines and begins to hiss.

"Hold on, you! You're the guest here. Get some manners, or else!" I bat at the crate, and he backs down. I open the door just wide enough to set his crate inside and leave the other items on the porch for the time being. Georgie circles the crate. They try to touch noses through the mesh. I take that as a good sign, and unzip the front flap. She backs up and scoots down into her rabbit stance to better see what's coming out of that carrier. He pounces her way, and they rub noses freely. He pounces again, tries to catch her tail, and they are off. Chasing, stopping, rolling, hissing, batting, hair flying, and ears pressed back. It's going to be a long afternoon.

I jump in and catch him, push him gently into the carrier, and zip him up. The guest bathroom is the best option for his new home, I decide as I close the door. Georgie is as mad as a cat can be, under my bed, right in the center, where I can't reach her.

"Come on out, Georgie. It's okay now. I put him in another room. You're safe!"

She doesn't move. She glares at me in that cat way. I check on her every 15 minutes or so, alternating between checking on her and him. I remember all the stuff I left on the porch, and bring it in so I can make him comfortable in his new bathroom home.

Finally, I can nibble on a snack myself and try to get to bed with my own sweet cat still under it, refusing to speak to me. I don't blame her at all, especially when Rascal starts howling once again at around 2 AM. I decide to wait him out. He has everything in that bathroom that a cat could need. By 2:18 AM, we have both had enough. I decide to free him and let the best cat win. I'm going to have to leave them together when I go to work in just a few short hours. I might as well see what happens now, as I'm wide awake with two stressed cats.

I open the bathroom door. He flies out much like he did when I first met him. He's like a speed demon, and Georgie is chasing right behind him. They both race around the rooms, down the hall, through the kitchen, and back again. Finally, he ducks into the pantry and squeezes behind my case of water for emergency use only. Georgie sits back on her haunches and keeps guard. We look at each other. She meows softly as if to say I've got this, go back to bed. Even if that is not what she means, I go back to my bed to rest until the alarm goes off. After work, I will go to the hospital for my shift with Daddy.

An abrupt noise edges into my brain, and I sit straight up. Realizing that noise is my alarm and means I have to get up, I softly moan. I put food and water in Georgie's bowl and watch her eat. Rascal comes sneaking out, determined to have what she has. I grab him before he has time to run and take him to the guest bathroom for his meal. I shut the door behind him and take my shower. As soon as I'm finished, I open the door to release him. This time, he walks out and sniffs around at my feet. I almost touch his head, but he ducks under and sprints away in a series of steady hops. He and Georgie stare each other down. I can't deal with all this cat energy. I finish my routine and let them work things out. I hope I have a house when I get back home. I decide to use my lunch hour to come by here and see how much destruction they have managed to do. Maybe I will only work a half day and come home for a nap before I go to the hospital.

I leave without looking back. Meadow texted that Daddy is going to be moved to a regular room sometime today. He was awake and talking to her for a bit last night. All sounds good to me.

When I get to the office, I let my boss know I'm leaving at noon. Clacinda and I work through the plan I outlined yesterday. She assures me they can handle the client and all that needs to be communicated. She promises to text or call if she can't. I leave right on time and call Oakley. He gives me the room number for Daddy and an update on how he is doing.

"He's still not able to use his legs. They are trying to determine if he can eat or swallow, or if he just doesn't want to eat at all. He seems to reset in his mind each day as if the day before never happened. He doesn't remember that he can't walk. It's so sad, Via. It's so hard to see him like this."

"I can't imagine. I just can't. I should be there when his dinner comes today. Maybe I can coax him to eat."

We talked a few more minutes about the kitten, Caleb, and Meadow, just idle talk like we used to do before the stroke, before the EMS, before this latest setback. It feels like a month has passed since our Thanksgiving.

I listen at my door to hear any sound of cat-fighting before I walk in. All is quiet. I close the door behind me and go from room to room. I find Georgie on my bed, fast asleep with a contented look on her face. I find Rascal behind the case of emergency water, curled up, sound asleep. Well, then. I plop down on my bed, determined to nap for one hour before I leave again. I have no trouble accomplishing that with my two sleeping cats in the house.

Once again, my phone wakes me up, this time with a text from Tony sent 45 minutes ago.

'Call me when you get a minute. Too much to text.'

I take a chance before the phone anxiety can creep in any further. He answers on the third ring.

"Hey, Vinca, listen, I'm at work, so I need to get right to the point. Jane Doe left the hospital sometime in the night. She did not get the message about the kitten. I know you've got a lot on you right now, but I felt like you would want to know this."

"Oh, wow! Yes, thank you for letting me know. All the antics, the vet bill, and the lack of sleep somehow made me feel like the heroine of the day for Jane Doe's cat. I almost imagined...Okay, I did imagine a headline feel-good storyline minute at the end of the local news. Man, oh, man. I'm at a loss, which almost never happens to me. I always have a plan B, C, and D."

"How is your dad? Any change?"

"He was moved to a regular room today. He did have a stroke. He can't move one of his legs and the other has a boot for his ankle, but he can talk," My voice cracks and the tears begin. "Ah, I'm a wreck...anyway, thanks for letting me know. I know you're working. I literally can't think right now. I'll keep in touch."

"I'm so sorry for your family. This is a lot. I will check on you later if that's okay." Tony replies.

"Thank you, Tony. That will be fine. Bye, for now."

I leave as soon as the cats seem like they will survive several more hours on their own. I know Georgie has her share of hiding places she can escape to if Rascal is too demanding or loud. Plus, she is four times his size. What in the world could have happened to Jane Doe, aka CW, which seems more fitting now since she has disappeared? Something tells me she's looking for the kitten. Something tells me she'll go back to where she was before. That's at least a ten-mile hike from TriCare Hospital to the park near my office. Maybe I can drive the route now. But Tony said she left in the night. She could be anywhere along it. How long would it take an old woman to walk ten miles? I hope she got dressed before she left and is not wandering around in a hospital gown.

I'm exhausted from being the cat rescue home, from worrying about Daddy, and worst case scenario for him. I can't call Meadow yet. I turn up the music, roll down the windows, and let the tears, which turn into sobs, release just as I cross the Ashley River. What surreal universe did I land in?

The halls of the hospital echo my footsteps, and the mirror-like tiles gleam in antiseptic cleanliness. The plant atrium in the center of the entryway, lined with palm trees, offers a relaxing place for the staff and visitors to come. I'm as keyed up as I can be.

I punch the elevator button and ride up with a stop at each floor as people get on and off. There's a man with a blue balloon bouquet who can't stop smiling. A woman gets on and wipes away tears. Staff members talk in medical code, so that we who share the elevator can't decipher any personal information. The comings and goings of life, trials and celebrations, hardships and agonies, whirl around me. I spin in a vortex of all of this. I almost push past the others to get off at my floor. A kind-looking man walks by with a therapy dog.

"Would you like to pet him?" he asks.

"No, I'm more of a cat person," I answer, wondering what made him ask me.

His dog has other plans. He sits and places his large curly head under my hand. I laugh a little and pat him a few times. He looks at me with these soulful eyes. Before I know it, I'm scratching behind his ears and calling him a good dog. His owner smiles.

"Thank you. I had no idea I even needed that," I say.

"That's why we make a great team. I look for the people who need to love on him, and he lets them so that he can love them back. I hope your patient is going to be okay soon," he adds.

I walk into Daddy's room, and he's asleep. His face is relaxed, and he looks so peaceful. I see the notepad near the visitor's chair and catch up with what Oakley found out. I read he has trouble remembering anything but the present moment.

"Well, Flower Bud, I'm so glad to see you. It's been such a long time since you came around!"

I stand up and clasp his hand that's not connected to an IV. I smooth his hair down and make a mental note to find a comb.

"Hey, Daddy! So good to see you!" I make myself pause before I add that I was just here, was just at his house, just spent Thanksgiving there. This is so hard!

"I hope Caleb can come soon. I still need to be sure he learns how to throw that cast net. When do you think he can come?"

"Soon, Daddy, very soon."

"Do you mind if I rest a little bit? I feel exhausted right now," he says. I adjust the blanket around him and run my fingers across his forehead just like he used to do for me. The heart of me, and the depth of my core feelings, fight with each other as I struggle to stay standing. Oh, how I love this man. Does he have any idea how much? Have I taken the time lately to let him know? As I watch, his breathing slows, his face relaxes. He falls into a peaceful sleep.

I sit on the edge of the visitor chair. Pulling out my phone, the magnitude of the fragility of life hits me hard. How self-centered have I been? I may not be able to change a thing about my father lying beside me, but I can begin to change how I react to everyone.

I check in with Clacinda and take the time to thank her. When have I done that lately? I think back to Tony and the phone call. What do I do now? If I really care about the human race, I will try to find the CW. Yes, I'm calling her that once again for leaving the hospital in the dead of night. I imagine she did try her best to walk back "home". For all I know, she has a very nice place somewhere and even another human she can call to pick her up who hates cats, which is why she feeds the kitten and hides it in her pocket. I tell myself she's leading a double life and is really safe right now in that nice home. On the other hand, she could be walking in circles trying to find a kitten who is miles away, disoriented and single-minded, focused on the missing cat. I sent a group text to Tony and Meadow.

'At hospital. Daddy is resting/no change here. Can you drive from TriCare to the park to look for Jane Doe? Can you send out an alert, Tony? So concerned about her. So hoping my two felines are both alive when I get home. TKS.'

No reply from either one. I close my eyes for a minute and am startled awake by the supper tray being delivered. Daddy rouses up and begins to protest.

"The food here is not fit for a man of my taste. Flower Bud, get my wallet from my pants pocket, and run down to the corner to buy me a good, greasy cheeseburger," all the while giving me this sheepish look like we're accomplices planning to commit a crime.

"Daddy, look, there's chicken and mashed potatoes. You've even got some Jello! Just try this, okay?"

"So, you're not going to go get your Old Man, who named you Flower Bud, a burger?"

"Oh, no, don't start with the guilt trip!"

"I take that as a no. Well, here's my no. I will not eat this junk food made for babies, not men." He pushes back the tray and leans against the pillows with a sigh.

"Okay, okay. I will talk to the doctor and see if you can have some of your favorite food brought in. I don't want to argue with you."

I wait for his shift change caregivers to come in and see if there are any updates I need to add to the notebook for Oakley. The nurse tells me the staff social worker will be setting up a meeting with the family to talk about next steps and expectations, as Daddy's doing too well to continue in the hospital for much longer.

Before I leave, I check my phone and tell him goodbye. Oakley will be in soon. Tony sends me a thumbs-up. Meadow sends a heart.

I think about the next steps all the way home. What do I expect? Will he walk again? If not, how will we manage his care?

I enter my front door, easing inside—no welcome or attack by any animal. I call for Georgie, and she comes from the kitchen, hopping on cat feet, circling my legs as she usually does. I bend down to pet her, picking her up and holding her close. I need the comfort more than she does.

"Where is Rascal? Have you been teaching him some manners?" She purrs as she walks into the bathroom, where his food and water remain untouched.

"Kitty, where are you?" I hear a faint rustle from the pantry and follow Georgie in there. I lie on my belly. Two pointed ears stick out between the bottles of water. He's still there. I hear his meow and try to scoop him out. He backs up even farther. I just can't. The exhaustion of the day hits me like a need that cannot be ignored.

"Ok, I'm bringing your food and water in here, right beside you. Come out when you're ready. I am done. Just done. I'll leave all the doors open, so you can find me or Georgie if you need company. Tomorrow, I'll look for a pocket you can fit into. And, I'll look for your

CW. But what I need from you right now is to let me get some sleep. We'll all do so much better when I have some rest."

I really mean everything I'm saying at the time.

The phone, sleek and convenient, rests beside the bed. Wake-up time all entered, a peaceful chime to lure the sleeper into the darkness of predawn. Many numbers are stored in there. Some IDs, like yellow caution tape, say, "Don't answer this call." Others, like a taste of summer, allow for answering with a smile, small and filled with love. When the sleeper starts awake, the ringtone jarring and harsh, the news never sounds good. Heartbeat speeds up, hand groping across the nightstand, patting where the phone was supposed to be, knocking it on the floor. Both feet on the carpet, one toe touches the buzzing, jarring, angry animal of despair. The call in the night brings news no one wants to hear.

I roll out of bed and try to find the phone in the dark. It was Oakley. I stay on the carpet, leaning my back against the bedside as I play the voicemail.

"Daddy fell again. He tried to get out of bed. He's got cuts and bruises. They want to restrain him when one of us is not there. I'll call Meadow. I'm on my way to the hospital now."

The thought of my strong father being restrained in the bed makes me hollow inside. I hit the call button, and it goes right to Oakley's voicemail. He must be talking to Meadow.

I turn on my side, and Georgie curls up behind my knees. I lay there like a baby on the floor and waited for the morning to break or Oakley to call back. Either way, I remain stuck between the need for sleep and the need to be awake, rendering me useless.

Chapter 19
So Inconsequential

I drive all the way to TriCare and then to my office. All the while, I look along the roadside at every person who might be walking for any sign of my missing CW. It doesn't matter to me that she left two days ago. She could be along the route. She could be dead. She could be halfway to the park. I'm working myself into a near frenzy from sleep deprivation when I finally arrive at my parking lot. Great, someone's parked in my favorite space. I feel replaced already. In an attempt to hide my dark circles, I walk in with my sunglasses on. I slump into my chair and try to decipher the mess before me.

I pick up the legal pad and see a list of what has been done and what needs to be done. I almost burst into tears. The what needs to be done section is doable and can easily be accomplished in thirty minutes of good concentrated focus. I can pull an energy reserve from somewhere deep inside me and be gone before I have to interact with anyone today. I don't need anyone to ask me how I am. Even an innate greeting has the power to evoke deep emotion between what I know and what I don't know.

I'm 15 minutes in when Oakley's text buzzes.

'He looks like he lost a prize fight. A cut above his eyebrow, probably a black eye, and possibly a broken wrist. He is in X-ray now. He was confused, but joking with the nurses.'

I sigh deeply as Clacinda walks in.

"Okay, that was huge. Forget that 'what needs to be done' list and go. Just go. One more day will not make a bit of difference here."

"I really don't know how to thank you. To walk in here and see all you delegated, decided, and left for me is the best gift ever. Between my Daddy falling, the kitten rescue, and the missing Jane Doe, the lack of even an ounce of sleep, I'm a wreck. A true and total wreck."

"Yeah, well, the sunglasses kind of gave that away!"

I push them up on my forehead like a headband and attempt a smile that is a pitiful representation of any sincere feeling of joy.

"Girl, I'm not gonna hold back. You look like..."

"Shhhh. I know. I'm going to leave. I'm going to leave now. You offer me a chance to get out of here guilt-free by providing your expertise and capable hands to run this team. When my life settles down, we will talk about this and your promotion possibilities. For now, thank you. I got halfway through everything on the list before my brother called with, "Daddy looks like the loser in a prize fight and has probably broken his wrist. They are going to have to restrain him when one of us is not there." I do fine until that last remark. My voice breaks, the high-pitched voice takes over, and I dissolve into the tears I've been fighting all night.

She hugs me. A true, tight, caring hug, and she makes small circles on my back while I slobber and sniffle on her blouse. She hands me a tissue. I sniff, wipe, and pull myself together to leave for the day I just began.

I'm almost to my car when I decide to drive to the park. Maybe I will spot CW/Jane Doe and can tell her I have the kitten. If I don't see her, I don't. I tear off a sheet of paper from my work journal and write her a note.

'I have the kitten.' I grab a pushpin from my ever-ready supply bin for presentations. Yes, I'm always that prepared. I pass the park three times, looking as well as I can for her everywhere. No sign of her. None. I parallel park and sprint to the tree where the kitten liked to hide and pin the note into the bark. For all I know, she can't read. I tell myself, at least I tried.

I decide to go home and wait for more news from Oakley, check on the cats, and rest. Georgie's in the pantry again, and Rascal kitty's bowl obviously has not been touched. I squat down and remove the bottles of water one at a time from the case. I stop and stare at the limp orange body of the kitten. I will him to breathe. Seeing him motionless evokes pain that pushes up from some deep place in my gut.

"Oh, Rascal, please, don't be dead! I can't take another disaster. Oh, please, please, don't be dead!"

I gently lift his body. He lets out a soft kitten sigh. The relief courses through me, immediately replaced by dread, as I can clearly see he is very sick. Close to death sick. I call the vet with no thought of how I am going to pay the first bill, much less this one.

"Hello, this is Vinca Murray. I was in there earlier with a kitten covered with fleas, remember me? Well, he's sick, really sick. He hasn't eaten anything, and I just found him barely breathing."

"Bring him right in. We'll see you as soon as you get here, no waiting."

I wrap him in a soft hand towel and lay him in the small carrier. I drive to the vet as fast as I can reasonably go, not wanting another chance at a ticket for something I didn't do. Somehow, that seems so inconsequential considering all that has happened since then.

I walk right in, too afraid to take a really close look at him. Afraid it will be too late. I hope the CW is okay. Somehow, I need to know that this Rascal kitten and its owner are both okay. My sanity is now hinged to them. This feels like the proverbial last straw. I find my breathing labored and my knees barely able to move me forward. I follow the receptionist into the exam room and place the carrier on the cold steel table. I don't take him out. It seems so cruel to lay this sick baby on a sterile, cold table. Instead, I reach my hand in and gently pet his head.

He releases the saddest, smallest kitten sigh ever. I'm so focused on the kitten that I miss the vet coming in.

"Sure didn't expect to see you again so soon, Ms. Murray. Let me take a look at him," Dr. Johnson moves with her professional rhythm and examines him all over. I stand nearby the whole time as if I can't move.

"He needs to stay at least overnight. He's dehydrated. I want to start an IV on him and let him rest in a quiet place. How did he do with your Georgie?"

"They both seemed fine. I did leave them for several hours last night when I was at the hospital with my father. I didn't look too closely when I got home, as I was exhausted and just crashed. He didn't touch his food, and the water bowl looked pretty full, too."

"Sorry to hear things have gotten worse with your father. That is tough. Rascal may have had too much stimulus from a new place inside. Let's take it one thing at a time. Hydration and rest first, then we can go from there."

"Thank you. Sounds good, as I really need to get back to the hospital."

"Is it okay to text you with updates?"

"Please do. Thank you so much. For some reason, I was supposed to rescue this little guy. For that same mysterious reason, I'm supposed to take good care of him."

She nods her head and moves on to another animal problem. Her assistant takes him into the medical room for the IV and rest.

I can't go to the hospital. I just can't. I can't go home either. I find myself driving around the route from the TriCare Hospital to the park once again. I use my GPS and follow the back streets more like the crow flies instead of paved roadways. I don't even know what I'm looking for or what I might find.

I pull over near the edge of town and call my brother, knowing he will be home, and Meadow will be with Dad.

"Hey, Via," Oakley answers.

"I've been driving around town trying to settle my mind. How does someone fall getting out of bed when he can't move his legs?"

"Well, the Doc said he doesn't know he can't move his legs and may have had to go to the bathroom, thinking he was home. He would swing his legs over and reach for his walker. So, without any chance of balancing himself, he went right over onto the tile floor on his eyebrows and tried to catch himself with his arm."

"How does he look? Don't make it sound better than it is!"

"He looks awful. He's frail and weakened and confused. He can still joke and make us all laugh, so there's that. But it's just so hard. We still need to meet with the patient care expert to discuss next steps. Can you come on the day after tomorrow? That works for Meadow."

"Sure, I'll make it work. Whatever we need to do. Do the three of us need to talk first? I'm not sure what my expectations are."

"Probably wouldn't be a bad idea. Let's talk tomorrow around 4. I'm so glad we have each other."

"Me, too, love you."

We sign off, and I see a host of missed texts. The vet lets me know not much has changed. I'm relieved things have not gotten worse. Tony checks on me and offers to help if I need anything. I head back to my condo, hoping Georgie and I can sleep well tonight. I have a feeling tomorrow's going to be a long day. What do I need? Do I even know at this point? Why does everybody lie?

Chapter 20
Find Your Own Style, Child

I leave for my shift with dad at the hospital after making sure everything at work is covered. I check on Rascal, and there's little change. He's not out of danger yet and must stay at the vet's for another night. In a way, I'm grateful I don't have the added responsibility of taking care of him with everything going on with Daddy.

Before I left for the hospital, I walked to the park from the office parking lot to see if I could find any more answers to where the CW disappeared. I stopped in a few of the shops and asked if anyone had seen her lately—most of the answers I got made no sense. Not only were the workers certain they hadn't seen her lately, but they assured me they hadn't seen her at all. One guy remembered the posts about her, but most of the employees were college kids hired for holiday break jobs to earn some Christmas cash. Really, they were no help at all.

I talk to Meadow and Oakley all the way to the hospital. We want Daddy to be able to come home if that is possible. We are all willing to help with his care, and we can seek Home Health for him, too. Meadow and I can take the weekends, so Oakley can catch up on his work and have a break. The Home Health Care could be several days a week, so Oakley can work from home and not have to care for Daddy, too. We have no idea how to make any of these details happen. We are all in agreement that what we are outlining is the best-case scenario. How to get him from falling, cut and broken, to home again sounds like a long, arduous process. We'll try to set up the meeting and support each other on all that we have discussed. Oakley offers to let Daddy know what we have talked about in a big-picture kind of way tomorrow.

I park the car and rest my forehead on the steering wheel. I take a few deep breaths, determined to bring some light and joy into my visit with Daddy. The back of my throat constricts, releasing the tears that come and go so quickly now. I grope around for my box of tissues and wipe my eyes.

"Stop this! You've got to pull yourself together. You can, and you will." I sound just like my mother. I even use her inflections, as I offer myself a sad smile.

"Okay, Momma, I get it. I'm better than this. I can be the good daughter and get myself inside."

As I hit the elevator button, the same trainer and therapy dog walk up. He nudges his curly head under my hand once more as if he remembers me, and I scratch away behind his ears.

"Oh, hi, again. We remember you from the other day. How is the person you are here to visit? I think it was your father?"

"Hi! I remember you both, too. Daddy tried to get out of bed in the night and fell. He's banged up and has broken his wrist. I hear he is still able to joke and laugh, so there's that."

"Would you like us to visit him with you?"

"Actually, I'd love that! I think Daddy will, too. Is this okay, since we are not on your schedule?"

"We let the needs of the day dictate our schedule. I find the people we need to visit each day let us know when to come. As long as I listen and keep my eyes open, I can find them with no problem." We all move into the elevator, and I push the button to Daddy's floor. I enjoy a whole ride up petting that curly head. The calm and peace infuse my spirit as I connect with this beautiful animal. No wonder he's called a therapy dog.

We enter Daddy's room together, and the dog goes straight to his bedside. Daddy appears asleep, but the dog places his head under his left hand. Daddy's eyes open, and he begins to chuckle.

"I sure don't know how you got into this place, but I am so glad to have a new friend." He is so engaged with the dog that he doesn't notice the trainer or me. As they get acquainted, I stare without being detected at his bandaged eyebrow, the beginning of a black eye, and the cast on his right wrist. He's a mess!

"Oh, hello! Did you bring this animal in here? I'm glad, but I think you are violating a whole host of rules."

"It's okay, Daddy. This is a therapy dog and his trainer. We met a few days ago in the hallway. He wanted to come see you today after your fall and everything."

"Oh, Vinca, is that really you? It's been such a long time since I've seen you. How did I fall anyway?"

"We can talk about all that later. Um, I just realized I don't know your names."

"Oh, I'm Scot and this is my dog, Lad: the Brave. Nice to meet you both."

We all chuckle at the dog's name.

"I adopted him and his name. Rather than change it, I adjusted."

"I'm Vinca Murray, and this is my dad, whom all his friends call Charlie."

They stay a bit longer before going to see who else is on their schedule for a visit. Daddy and I talk about what he remembers about the fall.

"One minute I was in this bed, the next I was on the floor with pain and blood everywhere. You know your head bleeds a lot! It's been such a long time since I've seen you, Flower Bud! So glad you're here now!" I grab his left hand as he quiets down.

When was the last time I held his hand? I look closely at the creases of his knuckles and the wide, centered fingers. I open my other hand

and compare. I have my Daddy's hands. Mine are a tad smaller and less hairy than his, but the resemblance is striking. Even our nail beds are alike. Why have I never noticed this before? As I ponder these thoughts, more visitors enter the room.

"Well, hello, Vinca!" Mr. Grant begins as Mr. Malone slides into the room sideways, obviously hiding some contraband. Kyle brings up the rear with a stack of food boxes.

"I'm so glad to see you all! What have you got there?" I ask.

"We heard that Charlie's not too keen on the hospital food, so we brought him some real food. Crab cakes like he used to eat in Baltimore." As soon as he says that, Daddy opens his eyes.

"Did someone say crab cakes from Baltimore? Jacob and Grant, what are you doing here? Who is this with you?" Daddy asks. I usher them in and close the door to his room. I'm not sure if this is allowed at all, but I'm willing to ask forgiveness over permission. I forgot to ask the doctor about dietary restrictions.

"We also thought he would like a beverage. In fact, his favorite beverage is in this container, all covered up and safe, just like he likes it. Here, let's set things up so he can have a taste."

"No, no. You all visit with me for a bit, and Vinca can help me with the food and drink after you leave. Seems like I had a dog visit me earlier today, right?"

"Yes, you did! Lad: the Brave, the therapy dog came by. I'm so happy to see you three! I thank you so much for making the trip here to visit Daddy with his favorite food and drink. Friends like you are amazing.

"I'm going to walk down the hallway a bit and make sure I have caught up on all my work and home business. You stay here and keep him company. I won't be gone long!"

I check the office emails first and see nothing urgent, and move to texts. I read one from Tony checking in and see one from Meadow with a selfie of Caleb to show GrandPap to make him smile. I see a missed call from the vet. Before I can check the voice mail, a staff member comes up to let me know that only one visitor at a time can be in the room.

The three friends raise a cup to Daddy with toasts of better health, cheers, and bottoms up. Kyle guards the door to warn them when a staff member approaches. Their laughter gets louder with each toast and gulp.

"Whoa, you three! The nurse just came to let me know one person at a time in here, and I'm certain that means one sober person. Anyway, I don't see anything for me or Kyle to drink!"

"Of course not, she's our DD! You're on duty here, so none for you, but we'll have a huge celebration when Charlie comes home. You can bet on that!"

I see Daddy awkwardly holding his cup in his left hand. He looks happier than he has in days.

I herd Mr. Grant and Kyle down the hallway to the waiting area, and the three of us catch up on life while Mr. Malone visits. He comes out in a short time and sends Mr. Grant in, telling him not to tire Daddy out. I appreciate these two men more than I can say. Mr. Grant lets us know Daddy has fallen asleep, so they are going to leave the food and drink and head home. Mr. Grant asked the staff if they could heat the food later for his friend. I persuade them to take it home and put it in the freezer for when he comes home.

I sit and watch Daddy sleep. He's a little restless, so I play some of his favorite songs, thinking that might soothe him.

The beat pronounced by the heavy bass weaves around bare feet in the sand, on a dock, on grass, or on a dance floor. It calls to your Lowcountry heart center to rise up and move.

Your feet swish and shuffle, light and quick, a love dance between first date partners or those who have loved for a long time. Each one reads the movement of the other. With a subtle shift, intimate and soulful, the song fills out to embrace and let go, to touch hands, and release. To twirl and pass bodies around each other and back again. Love making and sensually alive in the movements of The Shag, the Lowcountry Dance, the State Dance. The dance was taught to me by my mother, one woman to another, with just enough sass to leave you confused but wanting more. I can still see her head thrown back in laughter and abandon. I hear her rich voice, "Find your own style, child. You will find your own style."

How many times did I watch my parents shag to the beat? How many times did I see their style so smooth and fluid? I ache with missing Momma. I ache even more knowing Daddy's dancing days are over.

He sleeps, and I listen to the vet's voice mail forgotten in the unexpected visit, and the bliss of not facing any more bad news.

'Hello, Vinca. This is Dr. Johnson. I'm sorry to leave this message considering all you are dealing with. Things do not look good. The kitten will survive the night, or he won't. I've done all I can do. Do you want to come and be with the little guy in case he doesn't make it?'

That was three hours ago.

I cry softly, so I don't disturb my father or slip into the space where all the sadness overwhelms. Maybe this was meant to be, because I can't get there now. It's simply too late. I don't even have a decision to make. It's been made for me.

I pray, "Lord, please end his suffering. Please be with the CW wherever she is. One more thing, please, heal my Daddy. I haven't prayed in so long, God, you may not even know who I am anymore. I'm sorry. I need you. Amen."

The loneliness pulls up beside me and sits down, covering me like a dense fog. I'm unable to move forward or go back. I sit instead in the sterile room with the faint odor of the liquor mingled with the lingering crab cake, sharp and pungent, turning my stomach into a mess.

"Miss Via, what do *you* need?" I whisper to myself. "Tell the truth. No more lying to yourself."

"I need to go home. I need to eat. I need to rest," I reply. I leave a much abbreviated note for Oakley.

It takes every bit of my resolve to gather my things, watch the tech restrain my father, and leave the room. The squeaky clean corridors reflect harsh lighting and sterility back at me like a cold, heartless machine. I ride the elevator alone. I walk to my car alone. I drive myself home alone.

Seeing Georgie, my sweet, reliable, healthy cat, at my condo causes the tears to release once again. I let her know the sad story about Rascal kitten. I make myself a PBJ with some milk and crawl into bed.

Georgie curls up behind my knees. I tell myself that no matter what happens to that little kitten, I did the best I could to give him another chance at life. I refuse to consider the giant vet bill that most certainly awaits me. I will deal with all of that in the morning. I fall into a deep sleep that comes from exhaustion.

Chapter 21
Confusion and Clarity

I send Meadow a quick text before she starts teaching, asking if she wants to ride together to the family meeting this afternoon. She responds with a thumbs up and lets me know she is only working a half day. I putter around making coffee and hitting the shower to take up time until the vet opens, and I can call to find out what I really don't want to find out.

"Hello, this is Vinca Murray. I apologize for missing your calls yesterday. My father is still in the hospital, and he fell. I was with him most of the afternoon and evening. By the time I saw you had called, it was too late to return the call."

"Hold on, Ms. Murray. Let me get an update. Be right back."

I don't wait well in the best of circumstances. I put the phone on speaker and wash up my dishes in the sink, tidy the kitchen, give Georgie fresh water, and water my plants. It has to be bad news after all this time. I brace myself as I hear her return.

"Well, he is still hanging on. We're trying to feed him small amounts of liquid protein. If he tolerates that and passes his waste, he will be ready for the next steps. I'll text you updates. I hope things improve for your father. You are going through a lot!

"We can manage with him all day, but if you can plan to pick him up before we close, we can train you. You can take him home. Let's say that is plan A. If things don't go well, I'll let you know plan B."

The relief I feel runs over me like a fresh rainfall. I had no idea how much I needed to hear that little guy was still alive.

"Yes, this is great news. Texts will be best as we have to meet as a family today to talk about our dad's next steps. Thank you. Thank you so much."

I call the office and offer to take on anything that can be accomplished remotely. I rotate between working and resting, trying to eat something from all the food groups and putting my condo in some kind of order. I know part of my coping skills when my life hits the crazy button is to create some order. The vet's office sends a text that the kitten licked some food off a finger and took a few droppers of liquid. Tony also sends a generic text of thinking of you and hopes today goes well. Meadow must have updated him on Daddy. He appears to be a very thoughtful man. The morning passes quickly, and I drive to Meadow's with at least my condo in order. All else seems to be so uncertain.

I pull up in the drive and admire the house she and her roommates have restored with so much love. She quickly descends the steps and lets me know we are going to meet Oakley for lunch so we can talk before we officially meet with the hospital group. She asked him to pack us a picnic so we can eat at the Battery in Charleston.

"That is the best idea I've heard in a long time! I have not told you of my latest adventure. That can wait! How are you and Caleb?"

"I'm worried about Daddy, of course, but Caleb is taking this very hard. He can't understand why Grand Pap can't walk, and he asks me a million questions that I can't answer, don't want to answer, or don't have the answers he needs. What is going on with you?"

I tell her all about the cat capers and vet visits, the CW escaping, and even my note tacked to the tree with a pushpin. We both relax into the retelling, and she sympathizes with me on the kitten situation. We ease into our sister relationship as easily as we breathe. She takes on the supportive role, and I am the needy one. We switch gears and reverse the roles just like that. We drive along East Bay Street, passing the historical homes and winding streets, as groups of tourists cross and stroll along the shops and eateries.

Charleston, a grand, elegant lady with tomboy edges along a lacy parasol, is a paradox of existence from the start. Its layout is easy to walk along and catch the rhythm of the Holy City. One of the oldest cities in the country, she was built with wealth in mind, and factions of European influence on the old cobblestone streets filled with cries of enslaved people. The market area, now a thriving, chic shopping and food experience, drowns out the cries of the people who were once bought and sold in the same building.

The Battery was built in Revolutionary times to protect the city from the British. The homes along the frontage road boast of style, class, and richness beyond what most of us can imagine, and gardens, unique and lovely. A masterpiece of architecture and style, palm trees intersperse, and the sea breeze wraps around porches and piazzas to cool the genteel as they sip their icy beverages of choice. Peel away the veneer, and the truth comes forth. A culture embraced by the founders of building wealth on the backs of enslaved people was not only acceptable to them but right and justified.

The picture of us Murray children is not lost on me. With our black mother and white father, we would have been ostracized, or even worse, in this genteel city. With us three appearing one white, one black, one mixed, we would have been even more of an anomaly.

People rarely give us a second glance as we sit here in these modern times. Likely, they think we are three friends rather than siblings, but there is no outrage, no danger, no indignation toward us. These truths intertwine, and the poignant existence of this city hits hard as a punch to the gut.

We sit on the Charleston benches with our picnic spread out and determine what we think will be the next best steps for our father. Ironically, truth and lies buzz all around us. If these grounds could give up their history, I'm certain we would be shocked, outraged, and cautious. From the start, the city impacted the nation with the first shots of the Civil War. In many ways, the citizens are still struggling.

"What do you think Daddy would want?" I ask.

"I know he wouldn't want to be put in a nursing home. I know that for sure. He has told me many times to take him out on the dock and shoot him if he gets too bad," Oakley adds.

We all look at each other and smile. He told each of us the same thing on more than one occasion.

"So, do we all agree that we want him to be able to come home? That we will do whatever it takes to make this happen?"

"Yes, we can say that now, but when the reality of his care gets to be day to day, 24/7, how will we manage? We can't put all of this on you, Oakley. We can help on weekends, but we'll all be exhausted and so weary. We've got to think about this, all of it, not just the valiant save the day children part!" Meadow reminds us.

We nibble some more and attempt to process what she said.

"You're right about all of that, but we can't possibly name everything that could or might happen. If we can agree on the next big step, we can work together on the details as they come up. As long as we can agree to listen to each other and hear what we are saying, we'll be fine. Can we agree to disagree? Even if one of us disagrees, we will listen and consider all the options. How does that sound?"

"Like a plan for now."

"Yeah, I'm good with that, too."

We pack up and follow Oakley to the meeting room. We're seated around a long conference table filled with one doctor after another, all working to heal our father. They each give a brief update on the findings of their specialty, the effects of stroke on a person's body, and what they would like to see happen next as far as his care goes. After they all leave, the hospital liaison lets us know the hard facts.

"Your father will soon be too well to stay here any longer, but not well enough to go home without a plan. An option will be for him to go to the Rehab Center for intensive help with daily tasks, physical therapy to strengthen his muscles, occupational therapy for getting adjusted to his limitations with his legs, and speech therapy, plus any other therapy he may need. The goal is to enable him to get back home. Another option would be an assisted living facility rather than going home. And, of course, full-time care at a facility that offers that."

"I know this is a lot. And I'm truly sorry you are going through this. What are your thoughts?"

We look at each other. Meadow and Oakley motion for me to speak.

"We want to try rehab with the plan that he will be cared for at home, whatever that may look like at the time."

"Okay, I will let the staff know. After they meet again, I will contact you. Just know, it will likely be early next week that he is moved into the rehab center, if not sooner."

She smiles and leaves her best wishes for us as she rushes out to the next task on her agenda. We sit there a moment absorbing all that has transpired and decide to drop in on Daddy before we leave. Oakley has offered to stay the rest of the day with him. As we walk to his room, I tell them about the visit from his friends and Kyle.

Daddy's bruised face, a watercolor mixture of yellow-green and purple, slack in sleep, gives him an eerie, ghoulish appearance. The little girl Flower Bud, part of me, is frightened and stops to catch my breath. As we gather around, I hold his hand again, showing Meadow and Oakley how much my hand is a smaller version of his hand.

"Caleb has these hands, too! Oakley and I got Momma's hands, I guess." At the sound of our voices, he stirs and smiles.

"Just tell me, does the other guy look worse than me? I never believed my patients when they said it hurt to smile, but I do now! You all are a sight for sore eyes! Pun intended. It's been such a long time since I saw you last!"

We don't correct him. We just let him talk about nothing important. Just a string of memories tied together in some convoluted way in his brain. Momma, his office, fishing, eating crabs in Baltimore, Grand Pap, and Caleb. Torn pieces, tied over again, knots slipping and tightening into a ball of confusion and clarity.

Meadow and I leave in time to pick up Rascal kitten. She offers to go with me as the vet is between my house and hers. We both feel somewhat nostalgic driving home, topping each other's memories one for one. We can retell the same story and recall the details very differently.

"I remember the boy that you liked so much. The one with the beautiful white teeth and smile. He seemed so nice to me. What was his name? Danny?"

"That's really funny, Meadow! Yes, his name is Danny. He was a control freak and was awful to me. He was almost 15, and I was 12. He beat up all my male friends who even looked at me. He threatened to kiss my best friend if I did not let him kiss me, and she was all together ready to let him, too."

"You are kidding me! Why did you stay with him so long?"

"Every girl in seventh grade wanted to be with him, and he picked me. I felt so chosen. He had this awful ability to make me feel beholden to him. He touched me, assuring me that it was fine, and I could not tell anyone. That he was only trying to make me feel good."

"What?"

"Yes, and I didn't know how to stop him. I didn't know who I could tell. He would pressure me more and more. I was helpless to stop him. Once, when I was very sick, I think I had the flu, Momma let him come in my room to visit me. I was in my PJs, feverish and so ill, and he was slipping his hand under the sheet to touch me. I hated him, then!"

"I am so sorry you had to deal with this!"

"The worst of this was that Momma walked in and saw him touching me. She nicely asked him to leave, then she let me have it! She asked me why I let that boy touch me like that, and if my Daddy knew, he would kill him."

"Oh, Via!"

"Finally, my best friend's father talked to me about him as the narcissistic person he was, and not good for me at all. I was finally able to break up with him. I have some real trust issues that stem from this. What about a change of subject?"

"Sure! Probably equally hard, but are you ready to take constant care of this little kitten?"

"I'm about to find out, right?

We head into the vet and pick up the kitten along with the instructions and cautions for his care. It's still touch and go with him. He'll need to be fed every two hours all through the night. I take him and his menagerie of supplies out to the car with a huge sigh. This day, like a heavy gray cloud, threatens to burst and drench me to the skin with flashes of lightning surrounded by the thundering beats of a broken heart.

"Look, why don't I pack up an overnight bag, collect Caleb, and we can have a sleepover. I can help you feed Rascal, and you won't be alone with him in case things get worse."

"I don't want to put Caleb through that if he doesn't make it! I appreciate your offer more than I can say!"

"Really, Vinca, I don't shelter him. Dying is part of living, and he knows we will all die, including animals, people we love, and strangers. I think he would love to be a part of a rescue, no matter how it turns out. Plus, I need us to have some time with you. Since we have been taking shifts with Daddy, we've missed our ice cream dates. Let us do this, okay?"

"Okay. I'm not sure what I even have in the house for us to eat! We can order out when you get back to my condo. You know, this may be just what I need after all."

I turn around to take a slow drive by the park, hoping for one glance of the CW on the roadside, at the edge of the woods, or near the parking lot. Nothing. No sign of her at all. Anywhere.

Chapter 22
The Hero and the Problem Solver

I settle the Rascal cat into the hall bathroom and make sure the guest room is presentable. I put all the supplies the vet gave us on the counter. Caleb and Meadow arrive, and we all sit on the floor. I hold Rascal all wrapped up in his towel. Meadow and Caleb take turns letting him lick the food from their fingers. We each drop the liquid nutrition into his open mouth. Faint purrs begin to sound from his weak little body. He must weigh all of a pound now. I carefully lay him in Georgie's old bed and set my timer for two hours from now.

We decide on what food we want and what games we'll play as we wait for it to arrive. The two hours pass quickly as we act like a family, loving each other as best we can. Caleb has inherited the storytelling gift and has us enchanted by his imitation of his teacher, classmates, and the antics of a first-grade classroom. Oh, how I love these two.

My timer chimes, and we repeat the feeding process.

"Caleb, you need to take a shower and get to sleep when we are finished with this feeding," Meadow says.

"Ahhhh, Mom, I thought you said I could help! I'm not even very dirty."

"Yes, I did say that. And, I have to disagree about not being very dirty! Look, you've got to shower and get to bed. I promise we'll wake you up if we need to. Auntie Via and I can handle things while you rest. No arguments."

She takes him to shower in my bathroom and directs him to the guest bed, so they can read together before he falls asleep. Their evening routine, so set and amazing, makes me very grateful she insisted they help me tonight. Oakley lets us know there is no change in Daddy's world right now. He'll return tomorrow midmorning and update us then.

Caleb is soon asleep. Meadow and I both take care of the kitten. We seem to need this time of caregiving. He's still just as listless but still trying to eat, still purring faintly.

After the first shift, we agreed to solo shifts with me taking the next one. I set my timer for two hours, and Meadow sets hers for four. She curls up on the couch with a good book. I turn in for a two-hour nap in my bed. I've decided that no matter what I find when that timer chimes, I'm not waking her or Caleb. Please, Lord, let him still be breathing in two hours.

I must sleep some because I'm awakened by my phone alarm from a very strange dream with Momma dancing away to her favorite beach music while working on a mural in the civic center of our town. Daddy is watching her with this evil intent on his face. I'm seeing all of this unfold, but I remain frozen to help, talk, or move. I startle myself awake with a jump, and my mind wraps around the reason my alarm is waking me up after only two hours. Rascal, the kitten, for better or worse, must be attended to.

I creep into the bathroom and begin the setup for feeding, making myself focus as if he is truly still breathing. I can't look yet to confirm, so I deny. I determine if I prepare everything that will somehow make it all right, somehow prove he's still with me. I pick up the bundle holding him, and he makes the smallest mew sound ever. I look over to the door and notice Georgie watching. She walks in and sniffs him a few times while I hold the towel-clad bundle of him in my hands. She lifts one paw and, with no claws released, taps him on the nose. I smile as he opens his mouth in protest or in hunger. I drop some of the liquid in, and he takes two more droppers full. I put some food on my finger. He licks it off with a little more gusto than I've seen since we picked him up. Maybe he's making a turn for the better. I clean everything up and place him back in the borrowed bed. I practically sleepwalk back to my bed and flop on my side. Georgie follows me and curls up beside my feet.

I set my alarm for four hours, thinking how wonderful four hours of sleep sounds. Meadow lets me know the next morning that Georgie was sleeping with Rascal when she went in for the next feeding. She can still amaze me after all these years. I'm hopeful but cautiously so. How can I really believe this kitten will make it? We try taking him to the litter box when Caleb gets up to see if he produces anything. Nothing on the first attempt. We make plans while Caleb gets dressed and brushes his teeth.

"Via, I checked with Oakley, and Daddy's up for a visit from Caleb. We're going to leave soon and go down to the hospital. We'll come back here later and give you a break with Rascal. You can go visit Daddy if you want to or just rest."

"Okay. I know he'll be glad to see Caleb. But remember to warn him that Daddy's memory is not what it usually is, okay? I'll let the vet know how things are going and see if we can make any changes to the feeding schedule now that he's perked up some. Maybe Georgie sleeping with him helped some. I guess she forgot what a pain he was when I first brought him home!"

I shower and dress, thinking I'll probably go visit Daddy when they come back. I attempt to write up a proposal for next week, but am distracted by all the thoughts of life. I planned to set out this weekend and find the CW. I was even going to ask Tony to help me. I have a nagging feeling that she's still in the area. She's still looking for this kitten. I'm somehow supposed to make this reunion happen for the happily ever after ending I long for.

I'll be the hero, revisiting the role I played all my life when Daddy drank too much and my siblings needed some normalcy in their lives. When Momma was in her artist mind and forgot to make food. When we ate whatever we could find, from cake sprinkles to bread with butter and sugar, for a treat. I would be the problem solver who made everything better, who fixed all for everyone. I'd save the cat. I'd get the woman into a shelter right away. She would find a job and housing and go on to live a productive life providing foster care for cats until she found them homes. I see a business plan, and I can make it happen.

Look at me now. Stuck here with the very sick, but possibly recovering, kitten. Unable to leave to search for her. Stuck here nursing the animal back to life while my father is wasting away day by day. Why do I even make any plans? The best I can do will be disrupted in a minute. I think about the day our lives shifted into an abyss of sorrow. The details are so sharp and clear, as if I'm watching a movie while in it at the same time.

"Vinca, you must listen to me. Sit down here, and let me talk. I have to say it all before you interrupt with any questions. Do you understand me?"

"Yes, I understand, but no, I don't see why you are talking like this. Momma, what is wrong? What the hell is happening?"

"I'm sick, Vinca, very sick. I didn't want to believe it when I found out, and I imagine that is how you feel, too, right now." She holds up her hand to remind me to listen and not ask anything yet.

"I have Metastatic Stage 4 cancer. I will live another 3 to 6 months at best. I can try some treatments that have horrible side effects. I'm not sure if I want to do that, or if I want to have all the best time possible with you four. This is my decision to make. I promise you, I'll make up my mind very soon."

I cry softly as she talks, and by the time she pauses, the anger and injustice of it all escape from me as the howl of a wild animal. She holds me, and I hold her. We rock back and forth, our tears mingling into each other's, unsure and afraid in this raw and tender time.

"I know your anger, V. Don't be afraid of it. Let it help you as you take all this in. I know you are my problem solver. You are the one who looks out for the other children and your Daddy. I am worried, V. Who will look after you?"

"You can't leave us, Momma, you can't!" I wail, and she tries her best to comfort me.

I shake my head to clear out the memory and face my reality. Who looks after me? What will happen to us when Daddy is gone? Have we made the right choice to bring him back to his house and care for him at home? Can we even do this? What will happen to Oakley in all of this?

I can only do what I can do. So much of what is happening is beyond my control. I detest losing control of myself, any situation, other people, any and everything. When I cannot control things, I feel myself dissolve into the pieces of a jigsaw puzzle falling to the ground one scattered section at a time.

Stop it! I have choices.

I can call Tony and ask for his help.

I can go visit Daddy when Meadow and Caleb come back.

I can focus on the plan for work. I can.

I texted Tony to call me if he can in the next hour. I pull up the work plan and manage to fill out the action steps needed for Monday through Wednesday when my phone rings.

"Hey, Tony! Thanks for getting back to me."

"Sure, is everything all right? I mean, considering all that you are dealing with?"

"That is a hard question to answer in a short amount of time. So, Daddy is likely to be sent to a rehab center early next week. The kitten

I rescued is hanging on to life with feedings every three hours, which is an improvement if you can believe that!"

"That must be tough for you all and your father, but he's improving, soon to be released from the hospital, right? That little cat is lucky you found him! What can I do for you?"

As I'm listening, I check off a mental list. Yes, for thoughtful. Yes, for empathetic. Yes, for nice. What in the world am I doing?

"Well, I have this weird feeling that Jane Doe's out there somewhere searching for this kitten. I have nothing to base this on other than a feeling, but it is strong and persistent. Can you report her as missing? Can a search be started from TriCare to the park?"

"This kind of thing happens a lot more than we like to admit, especially if the person is homeless. Her case was likely handed over to Social Services. I'll look into that and see what can be done. Unfortunately, you may never find her, as she could be anywhere or not even homeless, but suffering from dementia or worse. All that to say, don't get your hopes up, okay?"

Check off considerate and realistic.

"Thank you for anything you can do. I just need to know I tried to find her, that I did all I could to locate her. I hope to return a healthy cat to her and for her to be taken care of, possibly just lost."

"Okay. Can I put in a friendly reminder about our fishing trip when things settle down?"

I smile at the thought.

"That'll be a nice trip to look forward to with all that is going on around me. Thank you again!"

I don't have to wait long before I hear Caleb and Meadow coming up the walk. The sounds of their laughter and light-hearted tones lift me up. I open the door to let them in, and the best aroma around greets me. They picked up some Mac and cheese and chicken. Caleb and I both love this combination of comfort food. I hug him and twirl him in a circle as Meadow places the food on the island. She has a salad for herself and offers me half. We banter and dish out food as if it were any other normal day.

"As soon as you finish eating, you can catch me up on Rascal care and then go. Daddy was so happy to see Caleb, and they had a nice visit."

"Auntie Via, the therapy dog, Lad: the Brave, came into the room, and I got to pet him, too. I let Grand Pap go first since he's the one in the hospital. The dog's owner, Mr. Scot, said he met you!"

"Yes, he did! Isn't that dog great? He's so smart and really does help people to feel loved and cared for. I'm so glad you got to see them and Grand Pap."

"He didn't look as bad as I thought he would from his fall. He does have a really cool black eye! He let Mamma take a picture of us together. Can I show her, please?"

Meadow hands the phone to Caleb. He finds the picture quickly and passes the phone back to me. This shot fills me with so much love for these two males in my life. I ask Meadow if I can have a copy and drop one in my phone. I'd like to get this framed for them both and Daddy, too.

I brief them on the kitten's care routine and head back to the hospital. Forcing myself to only deal with one thing at a time, I focus on my driving. I sing all the songs I know and make up words that should fit in where I'm unsure of the lyrics. I release the stress as I drive. I think again about how Momma's last few months of life were. I remind God that we already had our turn with our mom. Could we not go through this with our dad, too?

My visit is short and sweet as Daddy is exhausted. I watch him sleep and see peace on his brow, a relaxing of tension in his muscles. His wrist is healing nicely and will not keep him in the hospital. I take a look at the various rehab facilities he could be referred to and try to sort out the pros and cons of each one. A central location would make things easier on us, but top-quality care is more important if we have to drive. We learn that he can have 100 days of care before he has to pay out of pocket. He will be moved to the first available facility as quickly as possible. In the meantime, he will continue with some PT and care protocol while here.

"Hey, Flower Bud," Daddy interrupts my intense searching with a soft, sweet voice. "So glad you could come today. I haven't seen you in such a long time." He smiles and takes my hand in his.

"Hey, Daddy! Glad I could be here too. I'm going to have to leave soon. Meadow's at my condo helping me, and she needs to get Caleb home."

"Yeah, he came today! He sat right here and loved my black eye! What a kid!"

"Love you, Daddy! I'll see you very soon."

"Love you, too. Okay, make it very soon if you can. I'd like that a lot."

I let the staff know I'm leaving, so they can restrain him in the bed. I leave before they come in. I cannot make myself see how my strong father has to be kept restrained in bed, because he's in danger of hurting himself.

When I walk back into the condo, Meadow and Caleb let me know the fun they had and how Rascal has improved. I thank them with a lump in my throat as I watch them pull out. I eat our leftovers before setting my alarm for the first three-hour shift of sleep. When it goes off, I find Georgie sleeping next to Rascal. She may be providing just the right amount of cat instinctual care that he needs. Maybe she knows the truth better than any of us humans.

Chapter 23
Seethe Like a Volcano

After an uneventful night, Rascal slept soundly. I didn't wake him up after the next three-hour alarm but went back to sleep myself for six straight hours of much-needed deep sleep. Today, I have to go into the office. He and Georgie will be fine without me here for a few hours.

As I arrive, I find myself automatically looking around for the CW. I can't explain why. What can this woman possibly be able to do or not do? If she were to show up at the park near my office, she would have walked ten miles. Or, she could have a home somewhere and gotten a ride here.

My mind needs somewhere to land to keep me from falling into shattered glass shards with all of Daddy's needs right now. My heart shrinks every time he reminds me how long it has been since he has seen me.

Instead, I focus on coping skills that will serve me well. First, no obsessing on something completely insane like "Where is the woman whom I clearly saw? Who clearly saw me and left the hospital on her own?"

Second, I will focus on what I do have control over, such as the business plan for my client. I push all the obsessive thinking away and unlock the office door. Climbing the stairs takes real effort on my part, as if all my energy has been sucked away into oblivion.

I sit at my station and begin to sort through the mess piled into Clacinda's neat arrays. I hear my boss's familiar footsteps, light and determined, on the stairwell as she arrives. I love working for a woman boss. I accept that challenges happen when two strong-willed women work together. We have this amazing work relationship and have had some very frank discussions about what is acceptable and what is not. This neat mess on my workstation is not protocol. I take in her laser-like beam as she walks by me, talking on her phone and waving first, then putting up her hand in a signal of wait.

I sigh. I mean, really? I force myself to take the stack of what I need to attend to and begin with one item at a time. When I'm focused on the pile and take care of most of the stack, she comes back in with a purposeful look on her face.

"Vinca, nice to see you in person. How is your father?"

"Well, yes, glad I could make it, too. Daddy has a black eye, a sprained ankle, a broken wrist, and has suffered a stroke. My siblings and I met to talk about our expectations for next steps, because he's too well for the hospital and not well enough to go home. There are all these nice piles I'm working my way through to keep some sanity in my life. Honestly, this just sucks."

"So sorry about all of this. Can you come talk in a few minutes?"

"Sure." I mean, what choice do I have? I wait literally two minutes and walk into her office. She doesn't hesitate to get to the point.

"We need a plan for times like this. We also need you to be able to focus on what you can. So, I'm going to put Clacinda in your spot for the next two weeks. She'll forward anything to me she doesn't know how to handle."

"So, are you telling me I'm done? I mean, this is a really crappy time for you to let me know this..." My voice actually cracks. She looks at me with her no-nonsense eyes of steel.

"Is that what you want? I feel like you haven't been happy in this job for a while."

Now that she has said those words, I realize how very true they are. I have not been happy in my job for a while, even though I am good at my job.

"I don't even know what to say. I'm hurt. I'm furious. I'm overwhelmed."

"I can see all of that. I, however, have a business to run and run it I must, whether you are here or not, whether you are having a family crisis or not."

I fight back the angry tears, feeling like every fiber of my being is in fight or flight mode, and neither of those options seems reasonable to me. So I seethe like a volcano called back to life, waiting to explode hot lava over the entire building.

"I think it's best if you leave now. Nothing has been decided beyond that you have the next two weeks work-free to be with your family, to think about what you want, and to make some decisions. Don't contact me or any of your team. We will consider this a sabbatical leave time for you. No hard feelings. You are hands down the best team manager I have here. I am sincerely sorry about your father." With those words of dismissal, she turns on her heel and walks out of her office.

I take a wobbly breath and reclaim my dignity. I will walk to my desk and calmly pick up my phone, my bag, and leave. I walk out the door. All the rage I have kept in check erupts. I'm in no shape to drive anywhere. I start to walk really fast toward the coffee shop, and let the pent-up emotion out. By the time I walk the square three times, I'm calm enough to order and head to the park to reflect.

My feet slow to a normal pace, and I find my way to the bench where I held my head back a few weeks ago, and let the sun heal my soul. Today, the cloudy fall sky is as gray as the ashes I feel all around my heart. I do not like my job. I really don't like my job. In fact, I can just about admit, I hate my job. I do like my condo, my food, and my car. If I let go of my job, I can't afford any of those things. Maybe I can look at other options when my head is clear. Why did I go into business anyway? My thoughts drift back into my eight-year-old world as I think about how Caleb will take it if Daddy gets worse.

"It's my turn to pitch!" Oakley yelled out over the noise of the pickup baseball game, all of our neighborhood kids were involved in.

"No, it's not. You have to wait one more inning," I answer, ever the voice of reason.

"Vinca, Oakley, come home right now!" Our mother's no-nonsense voice broke, demanded we drop everything, and run to the house.

"I have bad news. Sit here and listen. Your Grandfather Murray is very, very sick. Your dad is on his way here. Please, stay in the house and find a quiet game to play while he and I talk. Do you understand?"

"Yes, Ma'am," we answer in unison.

We listened as they talked. Grandfather Murray had a massive heart attack, and our uncle found him lying on the floor, already gone. Death visited for the first time, piercing and visceral, tearing my childhood soul apart.

I insisted that I be allowed to attend the funeral. I recall the lipstick matchsticks, the tissue boxes everywhere, the people in black suits and ties, the cold room with the sickly aroma of lilies overwhelmingly sweet. All of that, interspersed with the anguished wailing from my grandmother, pounded on my senses. In all the adult grief, no one saw my suffering, confusion, and pain. Nothing in my lifetime prepared me for the process of death, wakes, funerals, and burials.

The most horrific part to me was that the funeral was on my father's birthday. When we all gathered at my Grandfather Murray's house, all the Baltimore relatives acted like it was a family reunion with laughter, a feast of donated food, and lots of drinking. I cried bitter, heartbroken tears for my daddy, for his birthday forever tied to his father's funeral, and those horrible people who could laugh and party at someone's death.

I can't stay here any longer. I turn around to see if the note I push-pinned to the tree is still there. I do see something. My stomach cramps, and the skin on my arms rises in goose flesh. I go closer and check it out.

"Stay calm. Don't overreact," I tell myself, stopping with my feet tingling.

Yes, the paper is still there. The words "Everybody Lies" have been declared in rough childlike print across the message.

Chapter 24
All the Sorrow of the World

I stare at the words as if that will make her appear. A chill runs up my back, and the goose flesh appears again. I step backward one foot behind the other, turn, and sprint away. I rush back to my car, fumbling for the latch, needing the safety of the interior of my car to calm me down. I drive home in a daze. Like a pendulum swinging from one arc to another, from my job, to my two weeks off, to Daddy, to the kitten, to the CW, and all points between. My mind's on a trajectory of too much to process.

The relief I feel when I pull up to my condo is short-lived. As soon as I open the door, Georgie greets me with her distressed voice loud and clear. She dashes to the guest bathroom, stopping once to be sure I'm following her. The odor of sickness hits me like an avalanche as I round the corner. There, in a little puddle of fur, Rascal lies as still as a stone. I can't make myself go to him. I just stand in the doorway as the sobs break over me.

Georgie goes to him and nudges him with her nose. He mews softly, the best sound I have ever heard. I bend down and pick him up, wrapping him in a clean towel with just his head showing.

"Okay, Rascal. I can call the vet, or I can try to find the CW. See, you are very sick, even I can see that. You might not survive, no matter what I do. I want to let her know, for some strange reason, I didn't lie to her. Do you understand what I want to do?"

I'm not getting anyone's opinion. I'm acting on my own. I have to take a risk. I have to.

"Lord, I need some help. I'm asking for courage. Thank you."

I put him in the carrier and walk back to the car, placing it in the passenger seat, so I can see him the whole ride. How ridiculous is this? I don't try to reason out all the pros and cons. I don't make a series of plans from A to Z. I just go back to the park. I lift him out and walk back to the tree. We sit down near those roots, and we wait. I pet him. His breath comes and goes as his body weakens. I lose track of time watching him and waiting. I should have called the vet. How could I have been so stupid to take this sick kitten out here?

I sniff back another sob. It stops me cold. I would recognize that CW scent anywhere as "I need to wash" body odor. Her shoes step up closer. She watches us as if trying to decide what to do or not to do. I hold up the towel-wrapped orange ball of limp kitten to her. She takes one step forward, and both hands dart out as she pulls him close to her. She coos sounds to him, more than words that I know, but I can hear his purr. I stand up and brush off my clothes, unsure what to do now.

"He's really sick. I did the best I could to help him. I took him to the vet and fed him every two hours around the clock. He had a good night with my cat and was better this morning. I left him for a few hours. When I got home, this is how I found him. Something is wrong with his ability to eat and eliminate food."

She looks at me with those icy blue eyes and says nothing.

"I thought you would want to see him one more time. So, I didn't call the vet. I came to find you."

Jane nods her head yes and sits on the bench, cradling his little body. I start to pull myself together enough to walk away. She pats the bench hard and with conviction. I stop and look back at her.

"Do you want me to stay?" She nods.

I tell myself I am better than a person who judges how someone smells as I try to breathe and hold my breath at the same time. I suppose my sense of smell adjusts, because after a short while, I no longer notice. We are both silently absorbed in the kitten as he breathes less and less often as he gets weaker and weaker before our eyes. The helplessness of the situation increases my awareness of the need to accept what is happening at face value, with full-on recognition. There is nothing I can do to fix this, to make it better, to come up with a plan of action. I am where I am supposed to be.

When he stops breathing, she takes the towel and pulls up the edges to cover his face. She hands him to me. Before I can react, she grabs my hand and squeezes it tightly. She lets go just as quickly and leaves me there on the bench with the dead kitten and all the sorrow of the world.

Chapter 25
Crystal Clear and Engulfed in Denial

I have no idea exactly how long I sat in that fog of profound sadness. My mind was both crystal clear and engulfed in denial. I received a flood of awareness from God that left me grateful and filled with grace and peace.

All the lies ever told to me were told with the best intentions at the liars' forefront. Forgiveness from me to my Momma, who created as easily as she breathed, and never really intended to put me in charge of my siblings while she went into her art world. Forgiveness for my Daddy as he raised the bottle easier than he raised us when she got so sick. He faced her death with the only tools he had, denial and a bottle. The lies he told himself helped him to survive and to toughen up for life without her. He didn't mean to hurt me. The lies I told myself about them, about how I was treated, the fantasy world I lived in of "if only"... all helped me survive, made me stronger, and a leader in the workplace. Forgiveness from me to my younger self for all the times I refused to face the truth or to ask for help. As I hold death in my arms, I accept the fragility of life. I know why everybody lies.

My boss has given me a gift of two weeks free from work stress, so I can try to figure out my life. This is way more than my job. I see now one Crazy Woman and one orange tabby brought me to this point in a shocking slap of truth. What really matters is much more important than solving everyone's problems, controlling everyone's lives, and fixing all their needs. I must give up the concept that I am always right, if only people would listen to me.

What matters right now is I face the truth, let go of the lies, and find out who I really am.

Who are you, Vinca Murray? I'm one who feels deeply. I'm wise. I'm intuitive. I'm creative. I'm a daughter, an Auntie, a sister, a coworker. I'm a cynic. I'm a judger. I'm skeptical. I'm wary. I'm a mixture of all of these. I'm not certain what is an act or what is reality because everybody has lied for so long. The truth, the true me, is so small and weak. I'm not sure if she has a chance to revive herself and live in truth.

If I could have any job I would qualify for, considering all those above stellar qualifications, what would I do? One thing, for certain, hits me. I would not have the job I have now. The peace that revelation gives me shocks me to my core. Before I can go any further with this line of thinking, I know I need to deal with the present and this kitten's end-of-life next steps.

"Okay, little one," a new tear falls. "I'm calling in reinforcements."

I texted Meadow to call me ASAP.

"Is Daddy OK?" She asks as a hello.

"Ye-eassssss. It's not him, it's me," I sob out the story, sniffing in gulps of air between.

"Stay where you are, Via. We're going to pick you up. We can bring Rascal here and have a proper kitten funeral in the back yard garden with all the other pets that are already there."

"That's perfect."

As I sit and wait, I think about a dream job for me. What if I had unlimited funds to work with? What if I could be a boss? I feel the peace increasing and spreading as my sister and her beautiful boy arrive.

"Auntie Via, can I see him?" Caleb asks. I look at Meadow before pulling back the towel. He gently runs his finger on the kitten's head, right between the ears.

"Mommy says he was probably very sick when you found him. He died because it was his time to die. It wasn't because we didn't take good care of him. You know that, right?"

"Yes, buddy, I do know that. It's still tough."

We walk to their car. The ride to their home is quiet. Each of us absorbed in our own thoughts, each thankful for the other. We pull a shovel from the storage room, and Meadow shows me the garden burial ground.

"We can all take turns digging the hole," Caleb says. "Mommy can start, then me, then Auntie Via. Let's lay him on this bench. I think we should pray."

"Caleb, that's a good plan. Do you want to pray for us?"

"Yes! God, thank you for letting us have time with Rascal. He sure was cute. Take good care of him. Amen."

"And, God," I add, "take good care of Jane, too."

"And bless Grand Pap, and all of us, as we try to take good care of each other. Amen," Meadow finishes.

We place Rascal, wrapped in his towel, in the hole. Meadow assures us it is deep enough. The soft fall of the soil composes a dirge of its own as it hits the towel and fills over. Caleb finds some sticks and makes a cross to place on the top. Meadow and I add some Spanish Moss and some fall leaves.

We sing a song together that our Momma used to sing to us, a lullaby for a baby who won't go to sleep.

" 'Go to sleepy, Little Baby, go to sleepy, little Baby. When you wake, I'll buy you a cake, and ride you in a golden carriage."

What would I do without these precious people in my life? We walk into town for a snack supper of sorts and talk through my job situation. Caleb and Meadow offer me a chance just to talk and dream, and I find myself open to so many things, I hardly know where to start. I choose to start with the truth.

Chapter 26
Let's Be Real Here

Daddy has been moved to a rehab center near where he was hospitalized. His schedule of therapy is intense and keeps him busy throughout the day. We plan our visits when he's not actively in treatment. He's more limited than any of us realized. When we met with the staff, we set goals to bring him home. They assured us that this time in their facility will help us know just what he can do, and, probably even more important, what he can't do.

As I walk in the door for my time with him, I see so many faces of the family members that mirror mine. The forced smile that is just a mouth turned up to present a cheerful front when the eyes and heart see the fragility of life in every room. We try so hard not to pretend to be cheerful as we head to our family member's room. All rooms are shared, so the lack of privacy invades my soul. I suppose I project "What if that is me one day?"

Still, we have a good visit as I can roll Daddy out to the courtyard into the fresh air and sunlight. We sit hand in hand and throw our heads back like I did on the bench where I first met Rascal and the CW. I wipe a tear or two off and sniff as quietly as possible.

"Flower Bud, what is it? What is going on with you?"

"Oh, Daddy..." I can't even speak as the emotions take over, and I let out the tears. Angry tears. Sorrowful tears. Relief tears. Helpless tears. I release them all as I hold my father's hand, my hand is its smaller twin. He pats the back of my hand and whispers nonsense to me in that comforting daddy way. When I'm spent, I tell him about the little cat and the CW. I take on my storyteller role with the best of my abilities and give him a clear view of the funeral Meadow, Caleb, and I held for that little guy kitten. We manage a few chuckles and sighs.

"So sorry you went through all that! I have a feeling there's more. Look, let's be real here. I may not have a lot of time left."

I tear up again.

"No, no, I'm facing it, Flower Bud, I really am. I want to help you, all of you, as much as I can before I leave this earth. Let me, okay?"

"Okay. Daddy, it's my job. My boss made me take two weeks off while she put my team member, whom I trained, in charge of all my clients. She told me to consider if I'm truly happy there.

"At first, I was so angry. But now, I'm sure I'm not happy. There, I mean. I do a great job, and I have the ability to problem-solve and organize. But helping clients decide how to solve all their problems is not very fulfilling. The thing is, I don't know what my next steps are."

"Yeah, that is tough, but I think your boss has great insight. She saw something you weren't willing to see or dig into. Vinca, don't waste any time thinking about all your options with a spreadsheet in front of you and logical thinking! This is a matter of the gut. What if the sky were the limit in all areas of concern? What does your gut tell you to do? That's where you will find your answer. My advice to you is to listen to your intuition and make it happen. Be willing to do whatever it takes.

"If you need start-up money, you can sell your condo. You know the market for homes is great right now. That would give you money free and clear to get your gut dream in place. You and Georgie can move in with Oakley and me. See, there are two solutions for free right there!"

I laugh at him.

"Daddy, did you listen to your gut when you decided to be a doctor?"

"No, I did not. My vision of being a doctor came when I was a child, but I didn't waver. I'll tell you this: I listened to my gut when I decided to date your mother and later marry her. She evoked in me a spark for life. A crystal clear image of light and color surrounded her. She and I had our struggles, but we also had our joys.

"That's where my advice is coming from. She's part of this, too. Look at her creativity that you have in you, and let that lead you to explore and plan. I can feel something good coming, Vinca, I really can."

"Wow, you have my mind whirling! I don't have the right words... I can't even begin..."

I hug him as best I can and wheel him back inside, so he can rest before dinner. Meadow and Caleb are coming to sit with him tonight. As I drive home, I wonder if I can sell this place that represents my independence and ability to take care of myself. Maybe he's right. Can I live with him and Oakley? It was so pleasant over Thanksgiving, and we settled into an ease that I didn't expect. Can I handle accepting the choices he makes, even the ones that may shorten his life? One thing I do know, Georgie would be in cat heaven living full-time at the Spa. The best undiscovered answer will be found when I trust my gut with no limitations. What do I want to do? Where will the Lord and the truth lead me?

Epilogue

The morning sunlight reflects off the water as the ripples undulate on the surface, waking up the day ahead. Soft murmurs of voices walking the open paths, and animals padding on swift or stealthy feet, mingle with the aroma of freshly brewed coffee. The familiar staff greet the new people who have checked into Rascal's Retreat Center to restore, work off debt, reconnect with life, or volunteer to take care of the animals who call this place home.

Training is offered for therapy dogs and their owners who pay by giving back hours in local facilities. Vinca Murray and her siblings make a great staff of three. They run the place with compassion and care for all. The people of Adams Run appreciate the location, volunteer time, and donations. Word of the retreat center spreads from Charleston to Savannah and beyond.

Sessions on casting a net, using a fishing pole, and nature trips in a johnboat out on the tidal creek are all popular with the tourists and vacationers. A chance to sleep in a barn surrounded by therapy animals is another favorite for Youth groups and scouts.

Three seasoned gentlemen offer card games and storytelling around the fire pit in the evenings, complete with S'mores for those who want local lore and tales of history. Charlie Murray can manage from his wheelchair as well as Mack Grant or Jacob Malone.

Caleb and Meadow work the weekends and summer shifts with specials for the seasonal events like Christmas by Candlelight and Sunrise Spring Break. Tony can be seen helping with the horses, and Scot, the therapy dog owner, is a great trainer for the Center.

Vinca and Georgie have no regrets about selling the condo. They are content to live with Oakley and Charlie.

The best baker on the staff lives in the little house that Oakley built on the side of the property facing the road. She comes and goes as suits her. She leaves the pastries on the table with as much love as she can muster. Meadow and Vinca made her a monogram for the front door. The CW in white stands out against the bright orange paint on the door. An orange tabby follows her wherever she goes.

Vinca thinks about the words she spoke. Everybody lies. Maybe, they do. But everybody who searches for the truth will find it when they listen to their gut and dare to follow what they find there.

Acknowledgments

To write a fictional account of any story, expect parts of the story to be parts of you. No matter what you name your characters, places, and events, you will creep in around the edges, in the midst, or even take over a chapter or more. This experience was equally scary and enlightening. When it happened over and over, I let it. As the author, I can safely keep the parts of me anonymous. You can try to pinpoint them, or let the story unfold as I did.

The Lowcountry of South Carolina is a visceral place that runs into the bloodstream and fills the heart. The seasons merge into works of beauty surrounded by water, spartina, and blue sky-painted sunrises and sunsets that cause you to pause and praise God.

The sweltering heat takes your energy down to just enough to breathe while your skin is blistered by the sun or eaten alive by a host of stinging insects. The humidity-filled air closes in around you unless you cool off with the sea breeze of the Holy City or sit under an umbrella with your feet in the sand. It's a love-hate kind of existence. My fierce loyalty to my homeland takes all in stride, as I grew up in Charleston without air-conditioning.

Our small towns are overflowing, and our traffic is horrendous as so many people have discovered this gem and want a part of it for themselves. Change is inevitable, but you can't take away the stories, the beauty, the family tales and ties, and the way of the water. The way our table, laden with Lowcountry dishes from a fresh catch with red rice, cold beverages, and laughter, is surrounded by memories repeated to the youngest listeners.

This story was drafted over a 30-day challenge that I told no one about because I did not think I could write under that pressure. Once I started, I was amazed that by the end of 30 days plus another week, I had a draft. I kept my focus and storyline together, and off the characters went. Much to my delight, a story came together after a weekend of pet-sitting for my brother with my laptop, his cat, and a hedgehog.

After two years of revisions, editing, doubting, rereading, revising, hiring an editor, asking a beta reader, and finally hiring a cover designer, *Everybody Lies* is in your hands.

I think we all lie sometimes. We take the truth where we need it to go. Perhaps we lie to protect, to prevent, to provide, or to prosper. How much do we deny the truth? How much harm does that do? How do we navigate life with the push and pull of truth?

I thank my family of brothers, cousins, parents, grandparents, aunts and uncles, husband, families by marriage, children, grandchildren, and a great-grandchild. I thank my friends, mentors, teachers, pastors, church families, and women who stood by me and held me up in times of significant loss and intense lies. You are all in the story. You are all in my story. Thank you, God, who provides truth.

Don't miss out!

Visit the website below and you can sign up to receive emails whenever Cindy Barrineau Curtis publishes a new book. There's no charge and no obligation.

https://books2read.com/r/B-A-WADY-LVKGG

BOOKS 2 READ

Connecting independent readers to independent writers.

Also by Cindy Barrineau Curtis

Special Edition
Touching the Heart of God

Standalone
When the Breeze Whispers: Find Your Truth
Everybody Lies

Watch for more at https://cindybcurtis.com.

About the Author

Cindy Barrineau Curtis is a Master teacher, published author, and motivational speaker. Her career spans over 30 years in education, ministry, writing, and speaking. Her nonfiction writing offers hope and empowers readers with methods to manage life's ups and downs with confidence and grace. Her inspirational fiction offers stories that engage and encourage.

Read more at https://cindybcurtis.com.